Operation Morningstar

Operation Morningstar

Dorothy Lilja Harrison

ChariotVICTOR
PUBLISHING
A DIVISION OF COOK COMMUNICATIONS

Chariot Books
is an imprint of ChariotVictor Publishing, a division of Cook
Communications, Colorado Springs, Colorado 80918
Cook Communications, Paris, Ontario
Kingsway Communications, Eastbourne, England

OPERATION MORNINGSTAR
© 1997 by Dorothy Lilja Harrison

Cover design by Rick A. Mills
Cover illustration by Ron Mazellan

First printing, 1997
Printed in the United States of America
01 00 99 98 97   5 4 3 2 1

To Heidi,
who told me her story.

Acknowledgments

My thanks to Brittany and Lindsay O'Steen, enthusiastic first readers of the manuscript, and to Chariot's Elisabeth Brown for rescuing it from the slush pile. And special thanks to Editor Jeannie Harmon for making the final preparations such an enjoyable experience.

Table of Contents

Germany

The Route from Schwandorf to Waldeck
May 25—June 2, 1945

Witten
Papa

Waldeck
*Christa, Hanna,
and Irene*

Giessen
Train Station

Czechoslovakia

Wurzberg
Orphanage

Herrsbruck

Sulzbach-Rosenberg

Nuremberg
Prison

Amberg
*Frau
Schmidt's
House*

Schwandorf
The Villa

Introduction

Not everyone in Germany during World War II
(1939-1945) was "the enemy." While United States and other
Allied forces fought against the ruthless army of Adolf
Hitler, which had conquered much of Europe, many
German citizens became innocent victims. Among them was
a Lutheran pastor and his family, who lived in an industrial
area that was the target of many bombings.

As the fighting increased, all school-aged children in
German cities were sent by their government to live in the
country so that they would be safe. Try to imagine, though,
having to leave your parents for some unknown place
where food was scarce and you didn't know if you would
ever be able to go home again.

Near the end of the war, the camp in Czechoslovakia
where the "Mueller" children (not their real name) had been
sent had to close down in a hurry because the Russian army
was advancing. Those in charge of the camp tried desper-
ately to find relatives back in Germany with whom the children could stay.

The camp authorities learned that the Muellers had
relatives at a villa in Schwandorf, not far from Czechoslovakia, so that was where they were taken. This proved to be
very unhappy situation for them, because the two aged
aunts who lived there—strangers to the children—had barely enough food for themselves. They told them they could

stay, but that they would have to find their own food. It was in Schwandorf that the Mueller children secretly planned their escape and from whence they fled just before daybreak on Wednesday, May 25, 1945, when Operation Morningstar begins.

Years later, Heidi, living in the United States, wrote a high school paper describing the journey she took with her four sisters and brothers. That twelve-page story formed the basis for this book. All of the children are still alive today, although all but Heidi live in Germany. Katrina became a legal secretary; Rudy became a youth minister and, later, a high school teacher and, eventually, superintendent of schools in his community. Helga studied agriculture and married a farmer; Heidi became a nurse and married a minister; and Volfie became a technical draftsman. All have children and grandchildren.

The Mueller children's mother, who died shielding her infant during a bombing, was a relative of Dietrich Bonhoeffer, a Lutheran pastor like her husband. Dr. Bonhoeffer was arrested by the Nazis for being involved in an unsuccessful plot to assassinate Hitler. He was hanged in a prison camp on April 9, 1945, just one month before the war ended.

Chapter 1

1945

Wednesday, May 25, 1945

We dressed by the glow of the flashlight as I moved back and forth between my sleepy brothers and sisters like a mother hen. "Hush, Volfie," I cautioned the youngest. "Don't wake up the Steiners." The chauffeur and his wife were snoring loudly, but you could never be too careful.

Holding our shoes, the five of us Muellers tiptoed down the steep staircase: first Rudy, then Helga and Heidi, and then me, leading Volfie by the hand. We felt our way along the narrow hallway. Rudy tugged on the heavy front door of the cottage, and we stepped out into the cool darkness. "Now, run!" I said.

We raced as fast as our stocking feet would carry us down the lumpy cobblestone drive and straight to the black iron gate. My heart pounded as I picked at the rusty latch.

The gate swung open, and we were on our way.

When we dared to stop and put on our shoes, still within sight of the villa, there was no sign of lights or movement anywhere.

"I hope the aunts are still sleeping," said Helga, looking nervously over her shoulder. She had just turned twelve and was always fretting.

"You know those old women never get up this early," I said, flinging back my braids. "Besides, even if they did, they'd never think we'd leave without saying good-bye." I adjusted my knapsack and stood up. "Come on, let's go."

"I'm glad we didn't say good-bye," said Helga, from behind Rudy and me. "Those old grouches!"

Rudy shook his head. "You'd be grouchy too," he said, "if five kids were dumped on your doorstep like we were on theirs."

Sometimes Rudy seemed older than thirteen. Even though I was a year and a half older than he, I hadn't even thought about how the aunts might have felt about our arriving like that. They hardly had enough for themselves. "I just wish we could have thanked them," Rudy added.

"Thanked them for what?" I asked, kicking a stone in my path. "Having to scrounge around for our own food? Sleeping in that drafty old loft?"

"Katrina," he said, "you know there wasn't any other place for us once the American soldiers took over their house."

"Well, I still think they were mean."

Heidi spoke up. She was ten, sentimental, and homesick

more often than the rest of us. "Wait till Papa hears about it," she said. At that we all fell silent. Did we dare hope that Papa was still in Witten? That he was even alive?

Helga fell into step alongside me. "What if we get up to Waldeck too late?" she asked. Waldeck was the little town where our three youngest sisters were staying. Some friends were taking care of them for Papa while he stayed in Witten. Waldeck was safer than Witten.

"What do you mean, 'too late'?" said Volfie.

I glanced over at him as we walked. "We'll get there in time, Volfie," I said. "Aunt Brigette said they weren't leaving for America until June first."

"That's next week, Katrina," said Helga.

I tossed my head. "I know," I said, "but we'll make it if we keep going."

We hurried on through the center of town. Even in the semi-darkness we could see that Schwandorf, like most of our cities, was pitted and piled with debris from the bombings. Volfie clung to my hand as we passed the shadowy rubble. "Remember how scared we were in the cellar?" he asked.

I nodded. Already the events were becoming a legend to us. "We were lucky to come out alive," I said. A chill ran down my back as I remembered the sound of the bombs whistling overhead. The last air raid had been the worst. The house shook violently, and window glass flew everywhere. We all clung to each other, screaming in the darkness. In the morning all the walls were cracked, and gray dust covered everything in the house. Outside, deep holes pitted the grounds of the villa, but miraculously all the buildings were still standing.

Now, though, just a few weeks later, the bombings had ceased. World War II had ended, and we could finally go home.

Soon we left Schwandorf behind and escaped to the green Bavarian countryside. A poppy-red sliver of sun peeked up over the horizon, revealing tree-covered hills in the distance. The arching sky was deep blue and cloud-less—perfect weather for the long hike ahead of us.

We walked along in twos and threes, swinging arm-in-arm down the road. Suddenly Heidi let go and started walking backward, shading her eyes. "Look!" she said, pointing. "Just like we planned: Operation Morningstar!"

We looked. The planet Venus—the morning star—hung suspended in the eastern sky like a sparkling white diamond against blue velvet. Everyone raised a fist and shouted, "Yea!" Everyone except me. My stomach tightened as I faked a smile. Over four hundred kilometers to go—days and days of traveling—and no turning back.

Whenever we stopped to rest, we rechecked our map. I had penciled in the route all the way up to Waldeck in central Germany. Amberg, our destination for that first day, lay about twenty kilometers to the northwest. We had to get there, even if we walked all day. And we did. Late that afternoon we dragged ourselves into the little village.

At an intersection, Volfie suddenly plunked down on a curb. "I can't walk anymore, Trina," he said, dropping his tousled head onto his knees. He was only nine years old, and he looked so small and wilted I wanted to gather him into my arms. It was my job, though, to keep our spirits up.

Chapter One

"It's time we all took a rest, Volfie," I said. I sat down alongside him and circled my arm around his shoulders. "Just a little bit farther, and we'll find a place to stay—I hope. Then you can rest all night."

The others silently joined us on the curb, too tired to even speak. Before the war, passersby would have stared—our undernourished bodies were dressed in oversized clothes, and it had been many weeks since the boys had had haircuts. But now no one paid any attention to us.

"I'm hungry," Volfie whined.

"I know. We all are. But first we have to find a place to stay." I hadn't the vaguest idea where that would be, but if we could just find an abandoned house or something. . . .

A heavyset woman lugging a gingham-covered shopping basket came hustling along the sidewalk. She stopped right behind us.

"Do you need help?" she asked.

I looked up at her from over my shoulder. Her face was marshmallow-soft like our grandmother's used to be, and a large brimmed straw hat framed her gray head like a halo. As her crinkly eyes looked us over, I felt embarrassed to be so ragged looking, dressed in hand-me-downs from the camp. I scrambled to my feet.

To my surprise, I found myself looking down at the woman, for she was no taller than Rudy. A faded green shawl draped her shoulders, and the hem of her brown wool skirt grazed her high-topped shoes.

"Can I help you?" she asked again.

"Yes, please, we need a place to stay," I said. Then I added, "Just for tonight," as if that made it a simple matter.

Rudy and Helga lined up beside me, and the younger two stood half-hidden behind my skirt.

"You are alone?" she asked, watching us closely.

"Yes," said Rudy. "We're on our way to our little sisters," he added, as casually as if they lived around the corner. He tossed back a shock of blond hair and squinted at her in the late afternoon sun.

"You have yet another sister?" she asked, smiling.

"Three more," giggled Heidi.

"Christa, Hanna, and Irene," said Volfie. At least he still remembered their names.

The woman listened as Rudy explained, "Some people are taking care of them for our father."

I interrupted, "But only until next week. Then they're being sent to the United States."

"The United States! How do you know that?"

"Our aunts told us," I said. We weren't sure how they had heard about it. In my worst moments I wondered if they'd made it up, hoping we'd leave the villa. But how could we ignore even a rumor if it offered some hope?

"Where are your sisters staying?" asked the woman.

"In Waldeck."

"Waldeck! That's terribly far from here. You're not trying to go all the way up there by yourselves?"

"We have to," I said, and everyone nodded with me.

Then Rudy said, "If we find our sisters, then maybe we can find our father." He explained that Papa, a Lutheran pastor, had stayed with his church in Witten. As an industrial center, Witten had been the target of many bombings. Papa had to live there, but at least his children could be safe.

We hadn't heard from him, though, since the post office was bombed, so we weren't sure where he was now. Telephone service had ended, and transportation had almost come to a halt.

"But where is your mother?" asked the woman.

"She died last year," I said, swallowing hard. Papa's telegram telling us about the bombing was the last time we'd heard from him.

The woman looked around at each of us. "Look," she said gently, "my name is Frau Schmidt, and you may stay in my house tonight. I have food and extra beds, and I live just down the street."

Later, while we feasted on Frau Schmidt's vegetable soup and thick slices of warm rye bread, she told us how she had been widowed ten years earlier and that one of her sons had died defending Germany after the Allies invaded Normandy.

"Thank God I had a good pension," she said, "and a daughter on a farm. If it weren't for that, I don't know what I would have done for food." She shoved back her chair and began to refill our bowls from a large iron pot.

"Now tell me more about yourselves," she said, serving each of us in turn. "I suppose you were in one of the camps?"

We nodded. All school-aged city children had been sent to camps in the country by the German government in order to escape the bombings. Because our other sisters weren't old enough, they had stayed with our parents.

"Our camp was in Czechoslovakia," said Helga.

I shuddered. Instantly memories of the hundreds of

children like ourselves who had been crowded into the ramshackle buildings flooded my mind.

"Everyone was scared and homesick," Helga continued. "The little kids used to cry all the time."

I was homesick too, but during the two years we were in the camp I had forced back my tears over and over again, trying to seem brave for the younger children. Now I couldn't cry at all.

Frau Schmidt set the last refilled bowl on the table and eased herself back into her chair. "How long were you in Czechoslovakia?"

"Until the Russians came," said Rudy. "Then the people at the camp sent us to Schwandorf because it was nearby. That's where our two aunts live, in a villa there."

I frowned, remembering the frantic camp officials who had worked day and night shipping children out at the slightest news of relatives, however distant. Schwandorf was just a few kilometers from the border of Czechoslovakia, so sending all five of us there had been an easy solution for them, but not for us.

Rudy reached for another piece of bread. "Our uncle at the villa used to be a doctor, but he died a long time ago. We'd never met him anyhow."

I set down my spoon. "Our aunts told us we could sleep in the loft over the chauffeur's cottage, but we'd have to find our own food." I twisted the napkin in my lap.

Frau Schmidt sat up straight. "Oh my goodness! What did you do?"

Rudy and I looked at each other. "We found work on a little farm nearby," said Rudy. "Earned a few marks that way, and sometimes the farmer gave us food to take home."

"And I washed clothes for the American soldiers up at the mansion," I told her, flinging back my braids. "They gave me soap and cigarettes to sell." I didn't tell her that I sold them on the black market.

Then Rudy continued, "The day before we left I bought some bread and cheese for the trip. And we took a little flour and sugar from the kitchen."

Frau Schmidt nodded and passed around some ginger cookies. Most of them were broken, and they were very hard, but they were the first cookies we had eaten in over a year, and they tasted delicious.

"When we had saved enough food," I said, "we stuffed it into the knapsacks we'd made."

"You made them?" asked Frau Schmidt.

"From towels and suspenders," said Helga, grinning proudly.

"Katrina stole the towels from the soldiers," chimed in Volfie, watching me as he spoke.

It was true. One morning after I'd finished washing the soldiers' clothes, I noticed how the men had dozens of towels, and we had only one. It was easy to slip a couple under my apron. In five days we had enough to make five knapsacks. Each time I took one I remembered Papa's instruction: "Thou shalt not steal." But taking a few tea towels was nothing compared with the commandments I had seen broken every day in Nazi Germany. I was sure Papa would agree.

After dinner, Frau Schmidt carried a lighted candle upstairs so we could get ready for bed. We girls washed up by candlelight in one bedroom, while across the hall the boys used our G.I. flashlight in another. We had no nightclothes, so we wore our underwear to bed.

Later, Frau Schmidt moved back and forth, tucking us into the huge, high beds as if we were her own children. I watched her and bit my lip. No one had tucked us in since Mama had last done it over two years ago.

"Is it all right if we say our prayers?" asked Heidi.

I winced. Why did Heidi always want to do everything just like we did it at home?

"Of course you may say your prayers!" said Frau Schmidt. Heidi and Helga folded their hands over the soft patchwork quilt. Their sleepy voices recited their evening prayer, ending with, "Let thy holy angel be with me, that the wicked one may have no power over me. Amen."

"Yes," said Frau Schmidt, smiling from the doorway. The flickering candle cast dancing shadows on the sloping ceiling. "That holy angel will surely help you find your family." She turned to leave. "Good night, my children."

"Good night, Frau Schmidt," we chanted in return.

The three of us lay still in the darkness for a while. Then Heidi said sleepily, "I think Frau Schmidt might be an angel."

"Don't be ridiculous," said Helga.

"Well, she *could* be an angel."

"There's no such thing as angels." Helga was quiet for a moment, and then she added, "Besides, she doesn't have any wings."

"Maybe they just don't show." Heidi turned over in the bed, and then she said, "Well, *I* think she's an angel."

Chapter One

They were quiet after that, but I lay awake wondering where God's holy angel was the day the bomb fell on the parsonage. And I wondered again how we would ever make it all the way up to Waldeck on time.

Far off in the distance, I heard a church bell tolling. *Who knows?* I thought, as I drifted off to sleep. *If there is one church left standing in Germany, there may still be an angel around somewhere.*

Chapter 2

1945

Thursday, May 26

Someone was shaking me gently. "Wake up, Katrina."

I opened one eye and was surprised to see Helga leaning over me, already dressed. Then I remembered that we were at Frau Schmidt's, not in the loft at the villa.

"You should see what's downstairs," said Helga, grinning broadly.

"We peeked," said Heidi, bouncing up next to me. "Frau Schmidt has breakfast almost ready."

I yawned and stretched. How could my sisters have such energy, I wondered, after yesterday's hike? But then, remembering the distance we had to cover that day, I flung back the quilt and swung my feet out onto the hooked rug.

"Porridge coming up!" said Helga, untying her

blond braids. She dug a comb out of my knapsack.

I pulled my dress from the chair where I had draped it the night before and dropped it quickly over my head. As I fumbled with the buttons, Helga moved to the mirror over the tall mahogany dresser. She stood on her tiptoes combing her hair, which fell about her shoulders like a fur collar. Both Helga and Heidi had soft hair like Mama's. Mine was thick and dark like Papa's. *Someday,* I thought as I tied my shoes, *I'm going to get my hair cut and curled like the women who hang around the soldiers. No more braids for me. After we find Papa,* I thought, *then I'm going to get my hair cut.*

I had done everyone's braids each morning since we left Witten, so I quickly did Helga's first, and then Heidi's. After they had gone downstairs, I did my own. Then I folded the eiderdown quilt and fluffed up the bed pillows, just as Mama had taught me. As I turned to go downstairs, I lingered briefly in the doorway, gazing at the cozy bedroom. Who knew where we would sleep next?

The dining room was warm and smelled like cinnamon when I entered. Frau Schmidt greeted me and set a plate of toast on the table. Rudy faced me as I slid onto my chair. "It's about time," he muttered, scowling.

I stuck out my tongue at him as I unfolded my napkin.

"Good timing, Katrina!" beamed Frau Schmidt. "We are just now ready to eat." She ladled steaming porridge into blue china bowls for each of us. "There's no milk of course," she said, "but there is a little brown sugar if you want it."

"Thank you, Frau Schmidt," I said as she handed me

a blue china sugar bowl. I sprinkled just a tiny bit on my porridge, knowing how scarce sugar was.

"I was telling the children," Frau Schmidt continued, "that a truck driver makes a delivery each morning at the marketplace near where I found you yesterday. If you get there by nine, you can probably catch a ride with him to Herrsbruck. That's over thirty kilometers from here."

"A ride!" said Volfie. "You mean we won't have to walk?"

Frau Schmidt looked over at him and smiled. "Not like yesterday," she said. "Won't be fancy, but it's the only transportation around these days. Should save you hours of walking."

"Yippee!" said Volfie.

I swallowed the last of my porridge and pushed back my chair, eager to get going. "What time is it now?" I asked.

Frau Schmidt consulted her watch. "Eight-fifteen. You have plenty of time to get ready."

She rose and stepped over to a tall cabinet. "I want to give you my address," she said, rummaging through a drawer. Returning with a stubby pencil and an old envelope, she wrote in large letters: Frieda Schmidt, 21 Morgenstrasse, Amberg, Germany. "There! Now you can find me if you ever need help again."

I thanked her and tucked the envelope down into my pocket, smiling to myself. As kind as Frau Schmidt had been to us, I had no intention of seeing her again. We had to hurry on to Waldeck.

At eight forty-five we strapped our lumpy knapsacks onto our backs. They bulged a little more than before because of the sandwiches Frau Schmidt had insisted we take with us.

When we reached her front gate, she hugged each of us Muellers in turn. "May God go with you," she said, wiping her eyes with her apron.

"Good-bye, Frau Schmidt," we said, and then we turned and headed up the street.

At the end of the block of gray stucco houses, several people were already waiting for a ride. There was an assortment of grownups—stooped men in ragged cardigan sweaters and women in *babushka* head scarves with listless children on their hips or clinging to their skirts. I wondered out loud if the truck would hold all of us.

A bearded man heard me. "Don't worry, honey," he said, with a toothless grin. "The truck will hold us. Question is, will it get us there?"

Whatever else he said was drowned out by the noise of the truck as it came rattling down the street. The wheels were bare metal, and one of the doors was tied shut with a frayed rope.

"What kind of a truck is that?" said Volfie, as it coughed to a stop in front of us. Above the cab, gray puffs of smoke floated out of a rusty smokestack.

Rudy smiled. "It's one of those wood-burners," he said. It had been years since civilians could get gas, so any trucks that were still running were now fueled by the forests.

The truck driver jumped down and surveyed us briefly. "Going to Herrsbruck?" he asked.

We nodded.

"Then hop on," he said.

The truck stood trembling as we scrambled aboard.
A pile of firewood took up half the floor space. The girls
and I found room to sit along one side, but Rudy and Volfie
stayed near the back. Soon everyone was wedged in wherever he could find room. The driver slammed the tailgate,
and in a few moments we lurched backward. Our ride had
begun.

We moved slowly through narrow streets. Then the
houses became farther apart until we were in the open
countryside. The distant foothills of the Alps looked green
and peaceful, almost as if there had never been a war.

As we chugged slowly along, smoke from the cab
blew back into our faces, making our eyes sting, but no one
complained. It would have taken us all day to walk.

Directly across from me, a gray-haired woman sat
watching us silently. After a while she leaned forward.
"Traveling alone?" she asked.

"No," I replied. "Our brothers are with us."

"But they're younger than you are."

"Yes."

The woman shook her head and pursed her lips.
"That's very dangerous, you know."

"Dangerous?"

Her eyes narrowed. "Young people shouldn't be
traveling without adults—not these days. Anything can
happen."

"We're careful," I said, flinging my braids back.

The woman sat shaking her head. I looked away so I

wouldn't have to talk to her.

Dangerous. Her words stayed in my head as the truck bounced along. Was I crazy to have suggested a trip like this all by ourselves? It had been my idea, but as soon as I'd told the others, they were eager to leave.

Every night during the week before we left, we had held nightly "war councils," as Rudy had dubbed them, to plan our escape. The five of us had sat cross-legged on a scratchy straw mattress in the loft, with an eiderdown quilt over our heads. In whispers we had plotted Operation Morningstar while the chauffeur and his wife thought we were sleeping. Rudy and I planned our route, and the younger children took turns aiming our flashlight on a creased and recreased map of Germany—our passport to freedom.

But now what if something awful should happen? I looked down at the blond heads of my trusting little sisters and shuddered.

Every half hour or so, the truck slowed down because the fire in the engine had burned low. The driver would jump out and run around to the back for wood. We liked that, because the more wood he used, the more space we had. Once the fire got going again, he'd start up the truck, and we'd be on our way, squinting through the smoke and longing for a gulp of clean air.

After a long while, the houses started getting close together again, and someone called out, "There's Sulzbach-Rosenberg up ahead." We had seen that town on our map. The truck slowed and came to a coughing halt.

By craning my neck, I could see wooden sawhorses placed end-to-end across the road. Two American military policemen in white helmets came crunching across the gravel until they stood directly below the driver. My breath caught in my throat as I strained to hear what they were saying.

"Got a pass?" one of them asked.

"For Herrsbruck," called the driver. "That's where we're headed."

"Sorry," said the officer. "Any vehicle entering any town in Germany now has to have a pass. You can get one at the town hall back in Amberg."

"Ach!" said the driver. "All these years I've driven this truck, and now it's passes here, passes there! I'm sick of passes!" He spun the truck around and headed back toward Amberg.

"Why do we need a pass?" asked Heidi.

"Because we lost the war," I said. "The Americans are in charge now."

"Of the whole country?" Heidi's eyes widened.

"Just this part of Germany."

Helga crossed her arms and thrust up her chin. "We should have gotten off the truck," she said.

"And have those border guards question us? Not on your life!" I said.

"Well, we've wasted a lot of time," she said. As if I had to be told.

I closed my eyes and leaned back, letting my head bump rhythmically against the metal side of the truck. I hadn't expected this setback, and I wondered how many other border guards we'd have to worry about. We had six more days until June first, when our sisters would be leaving. My stomach began to hurt.

At the town hall in Amberg, the official who gave out passes had gone to lunch, so we all got out of the truck and waited. When the man returned in the early afternoon, our driver had to go and fill out special papers. He finally came back outside and said, "I've got the pass, but it's too late to make it to Herrsbruck today."

"What do you mean, too late?" asked one of the women.

"It would be dark before we got there, and no one's allowed to travel at night. We'll have to wait until morning." He turned to leave. "See you tomorrow at nine," he said.

The other passengers wandered off, and we Muellers were left right where we had started from that morning.

Heidi pulled on my sleeve. "What shall we do?" she asked.

"I have to go to the bathroom," whined Volfie.

"Hush, you kids!" I snapped. "I'm trying to think."

Everyone waited. A couple of people passed by and stared, but no one spoke to us. I don't know what I expected, but I was angry that no one offered to help. What was I supposed to do? I wasn't their mother. Mothers always knew what to do.

Helga put her hands on her hips. "We'd better go back to the villa," she said.

"And face those aunts again?" I said. "Never!"

"Well, we do know one place where we can go," said

Rudy. He grinned, a knowing look in his eyes.

I nodded and pulled out the envelope Frau Schmidt had given me that morning. "I hate to bother her again so soon," I said.

"Katrina," said Rudy, "what choice do we have? We'll need that truck ride again tomorrow." So back we went to 21 Morgenstrasse.

Chapter 3

1945

Friday, May 27

The good Frau Schmidt once more had us rested, fed, and ready to meet the delivery truck when it came rattling down Morgenstrasse on Friday morning. Most of the same people waited again at the corner, including the gray-haired woman.

"I see you're still by yourselves," she said, looking us over.

"Yes," I replied, wishing I could hide from her disapproving glances.

"Just remember what I told you."

I nodded and tried not to think about what she had said the day before. When I climbed up into the truck, I managed to find a space near the tailgate, a good distance from the woman. Better still, I was farther away from the stinging smoke.

This time when we arrived in Sulzbach-Rosenberg, the military police came around to the back of the truck after they had checked the driver's pass. My stomach tightened, and I hardly dared breathe. What if they started asking questions?

One of the officers came alongside us. "Everybody all right back here?" he asked in broken German. His white helmet gleamed in the sunlight, and he was so close I could see my reflection in his sunglasses.

"Fine," we said, and I held my breath.

He looked at me. "Traveling alone?" he asked.

What should I say? Yes? No? I cleared my throat. "I'm with my brothers and sisters. Someone is meeting us in Nuremberg." I could feel my face getting red, and my voice trembled.

"Nuremberg!" said the American, shaking his head. "I didn't know anyone was still living in that pile of rubble," he said.

"Some people are," I replied. I wondered if he could hear my heart pounding. My mind was frantically composing a story to support what I'd just told him.

Incredibly, the officer took a step backward and waved to the driver. "Go ahead," he called, "but you'd better keep track of those kids. They shouldn't be traveling alone."

The driver waved back and started the truck. It coughed and wheezed and lurched, and we were on our way again. I closed my eyes, lightheaded with relief. Then I asked Rudy for the map, and I studied it closely for a few minutes. "I bet we could make it from Herrsbruck to

Chapter Three

Nuremberg before dark," I said.

Rudy took a look and shook his head. "Not unless we get another ride."

"Well," I said, "that's what we'll have to do."

At noon we were waved through the gate at Herrsbruck with no trouble. Herrsbruck was larger than Sulzbach-Rosenberg and the bombings had been heavier. "Just look at that," said an old man across from me, shaking his head in disbelief. "Half the town must be gone."

The truck wheezed to a stop, and we climbed out near what had probably been the marketplace. Piles of debris filled the square, and here and there people bent silently over the wreckage, pulling out what little they could from the mangled heaps—dented canned goods, boxes, and hunks of metal or wood.

After the rest of the passengers left, the five of us Muellers stood alone, staring at the crumbled buildings and bombed churches. The damage in Herrsbruck was the worst we had yet seen, and I was sickened by it.

Volfie looked up at me. "What are we going to do now?" he asked, twisting a lock of his hair.

"Get a ride, I hope," I said, looking around and trying to decide where to go.

Suddenly the door of the truck slammed, and the driver walked toward us. He pulled out a homemade cigarette. "Where are you headed?" he asked, striking a match.

"Nuremberg," said Rudy.

The driver cupped his hand around the flame as it licked at his drooping cigarette. "Don't know of anyone going that way myself," he said, shaking out the match and exhaling a puff of smoke. "Why don't you try the Americans? They're always heading out somewhere. Might give you a lift." He nodded toward the end of the street. "They're down there," he said. He looked at me. "Be careful," he said, probably because of what the officer had said to him earlier. Then he turned and walked off.

The American Army Headquarters was easy to spot. The U.S. flag was draped from a second story window of the old stone building the Americans occupied. Two dark green jeeps sat along the curb, each with a large white star on the side.

As we started up the steps of the headquarters, someone came up behind us. "Need some help?"

I looked back. It was a sandy-haired soldier with freckles. He spoke better German than the American at the barrier. "We're on our way to Waldeck, sir," I said, stopping at the top of the steps.

"Is that nearby?" He grinned down at us.

I smoothed my hair back and tried to sound casual. "No, but we're hoping maybe we can get a ride to Nuremberg. That's on the way." I clasped my hands, hiding my ragged fingernails.

"Let's see what we can do. Come inside for a minute." He pushed on the huge door and held it open for us.

Inside, we sat on a worn wooden bench and waited, listening to deep voices coming from the room next to us. Soon the soldier returned with two others. One was dark-haired and taller than anyone I had ever seen—taller even than Papa. The other wasn't much taller than I. They stood and grinned at us with their hands in their pockets.

"You kids are lucky," said the freckled soldier. "These guys are leaving for Nuremberg right after lunch."

The tall soldier checked his watch. "Let's see. It's twelve-thirty. Be back here by two, and you can go with us."

We all brightened. "Don't worry, sir," I said, scarcely believing our luck. "We'll be ready!"

Down the street we found a park that had somehow escaped the bombings. There on a bench we ate the cheese sandwiches Frau Schmidt had once again packed for us. Before the war we could have sat on the grass, but the lawn had been plowed under, and young tomato plants struggled to survive there instead. Just like back home in Witten, hungry people were growing food wherever they could find soil. Some had built shacks next to their gardens in order to keep an eye on their future food supply.

"Look!" said Rudy, pointing farther down the street. "Not a building left standing."

"Let's go and see," said Volfie, jumping up. We followed him across the street and down the block. The area was deserted—nothing left but piles of bricks, with a few walls jutting up from the rubble here and there. The insides of the walls were painted or wallpapered, and traces of what had once been staircases zigzagged along some of them.

Suddenly we heard footsteps. Two boys ran up from behind us and snatched at Rudy and me. One was taller and older than I; the other looked about my age. They were even more ragged than we were, and they had smudged and dirty faces. They sneered at us.

"What's in those knapsacks?" the taller one demand-ed in a rough voice.

"Clothes," said Rudy, stepping back slightly. My heart was pounding. My knapsack had our money in it! Heidi and Helga moved close beside me. Volfie hid behind Rudy.

"Let's see!" said the tall boy. He snatched at me again. I started to run. He grabbed my arm and threw me to the ground. I rolled over and tussled with him, scratching him with my fingernails and yanking at his hair. He pound-ed on my shoulder and tugged at my knapsack. The harder he tugged, the harder I scratched.

Out of the corner of my eye, I could see Rudy rolling on the ground with the younger boy. Helga was leaning over them, swinging her fists, and Volfie and Heidi were yelling somewhere behind me.

Suddenly I was shoved aside. "Forget it!" hollered my attacker. He ran a grimy hand over his scratched face and stumbled up the street.

As I sat up, the other boy took off too, clutching Rudy's knapsack. Rudy had a bloody nose, but he jumped up and followed them.

"Don't, Rudy!" I yelled, scrambling to my feet. "Let them have it!" Nothing in his knapsack was worth getting hurt. I stood holding my breath, with my fists clenched.

The older boy had disappeared, and as Rudy caught up with the younger one, the boy spun around and swatted him with the knapsack, knocking him off his feet. Then he fled with the knapsack under his arm.

Chapter Three

Rudy sat wiping his bleeding nose with the back of his hand. We all scrambled over to him. I pressed my handkerchief hard under his nostrils until the blood stopped flowing. "Bullies!" Rudy muttered into the handkerchief. "Now what are we going to do? Our flashlight was in my pack!"

"So was the map," said Helga, grimly.

"I've got the map," I said. "I used it this morning and forgot to give it back to you."

"But what'll we do without the flashlight?" said Rudy, getting to his feet.

"We'll manage," I said, helping him brush off his clothes. Then I noticed that both Volfie and Heidi were crying. "It's all right now," I said, hugging both of them. "Those bullies are gone. Let's just get out of here." We turned and hurried back up the street.

"Why did they do that?" asked Volfie, wiping his eyes as he fell into step alongside Rudy. "We didn't bother them."

"They were probably looking for some money" said Rudy.

Volfie whistled softly. "It's a good thing they didn't get Katrina's knapsack, then!"

For what little we have, I thought, *a few marks to last us all the way up to Waldeck.*

Rudy had a bruise under his eye, and my shoulder was sore, but other than that we were none the worse for what had happened. We washed up as best we could at a pump in the park and hurried over to the American headquarters.

Two smiling officers were waiting by their jeep, but their smiles faded as we came closer. "What happened?" they both asked, looking back and forth from Rudy to me.

"Met some bullies," I said. We assured them we were all right and agreed that we shouldn't go off by ourselves again. The soldiers' strong arms helped us up into the back seat, and I relaxed, knowing they would be with us all the way to Nuremberg.

And by late afternoon we arrived, safe and sound, in yet another ruined city.

As we drove through the streets, I could hardly believe what I saw. The ruins there were even worse than in Herrsbruck. Was this really Nuremberg, the city where Adolf Hitler had once proudly displayed his troops? I remembered a newsreel I once saw when Papa took me to the movies. Hitler was on a Nuremberg balcony overlooking a square, with thousands of soldiers strutting past and saluting him. Hitler, whom the Nazis called their *Führer*, was the leader who was going to save our country. Instead, Nuremberg, like most German cities, was a pile of rubble. It was as if a giant's child, tired of playing, had kicked over his towers and scattered the blocks.

"Look at that poster!" said Volfie. One wall still standing held a huge picture of Hitler which said in bold red letters:

LONG LIVE THE FÜHRER!

Hitler's mustached face, though, had been crossed off with black paint, and another long black line was drawn through the sentence. Crudely painted underneath were the words:

DOWN WITH HITLER! DOWN WITH WAR!

A chill ran through me. The sun was sinking on the horizon. It was too late in the day for us to make it to the next town even if we hurried. And how would anyone be able to help us in a place like this?

Chapter 4

1945

Friday Afternoon

The American soldiers drove us straight to their headquarters in Nuremberg, an ancient fortress that had escaped the bombings. We followed the officers up the steps, through an immense door, and into a dim and drafty corridor.

One of the officers nodded toward a bench along the wall. "Wait over there a minute," he said to us. Then they all disappeared into an adjoining room.

Rudy scowled. "I think we'd better get out of here and head for the countryside," he said. "Maybe we could sleep in a barn or something."

I shook my head. "We couldn't get that far before dark."

"I'm hungry," whined Helga.

"Me, too," said Heidi. "When can we eat?"

Before I could answer, the soldiers reappeared. Their smiles were gone. "Sorry, kids," said one of them, who had said his name was Larry. "No one seems to know anyone who can take you in." He dropped his voice and continued, "There is one place you'll be safe, though." He ushered us down a long flight of worn stone steps to a room where a uniformed man sat at a scarred wooden desk. Iron bars stretched across the doorway behind him.

"Is this a jail?" asked Volfie, staring at the long, shiny keys that jangled from a large ring on his belt.

"A prison," said the guard, looking us over.

Larry cleared his throat. "These kids need a place to stay tonight. Someplace safe." He explained how no one in Nuremberg could take us in.

The guard smiled. "They'll be safe in here, all right."

"We're going to stay here?" I asked, hardly believing my ears.

Larry looked over at me. "I'm sorry. It's the only way we can be sure you'll be safe. This town's no place to be at night."

I started smiling, and so did the rest of us. "Oh," I said, "this will be fine. Really, it will." *A prison! I thought. We're going to sleep in a real prison!* I had always wondered what a prison was like inside.

"I have to warn you," said the guard, unlocking the gate to the hallway, "keep your voices down when you're in there. The prisoners are strictly forbidden to talk to each other, and it is my job to see that they do not. So we cannot have a lot of noise." He looked around at us as we stood waiting. "Do you understand?"

We nodded soberly.

The two men led us down a dim passageway to the cell where we would spend the night. It was a small, damp room with two bunks, a wobbly table, two rickety chairs, a sink, and a toilet. The iron-clad door had a peephole up high in it, so that the guard could check the prisoners.

"You might not be safe here with the door open," said the guard, "so we'll have to lock you in." I bit my lip and nodded. "Meals come in through this little opening here." He pointed to a small, sliding panel halfway up the door. "Dinner should be along in a few minutes."

Larry and the guard left us alone in the cell while they went off for more mattresses. When they returned, they helped us slide them under the bunks. Then they turned to leave.

"I'll be back for you in the morning," said Larry.

We all smiled at him. "Thanks for helping," I said, "and for the ride, too." I held my breath just a bit as I watched them step back out into the passageway. The guard fumbled through his keys and slipped one into the lock. I shuddered briefly when I heard it click.

Volfie jumped up on one of the bunks. "I get to sleep here," he announced.

"Shhh, Volfie!" I said. So he said it again, whispering this time.

"I get the other bunk," said Helga softly.

"Well," I said, thinking fast, "four mattresses and five people means two of us are going to have to share one of them." I looked over at Helga and Heidi. "If the two of you will sleep together, you can have the table when dinner comes, and the rest of us will eat on the floor."

The girls looked at each other and grinned. "Breakfast, too?" asked Helga.

I sighed. "Breakfast, too."

Just then the little panel slid sideways, and someone handed us five tin plates and cups and some spoons. They were followed by a large bowl of beans, another of cooked greens, several thick slices of coarse bread, and a metal pitcher of black coffee.

The boys and I sat cross-legged on a mattress, holding our plates. "I wonder who's in the next cell," whispered Rudy.

"Me, too," I said. We could hear tin dishes clattering, so we knew someone else was nearby.

"Can I have some coffee?" asked Volfie in a little voice. He remembered that we were never allowed coffee at home.

"There's nothing else to drink, so I don't know why not," I said. So we all had thick black coffee that night, but no one finished it.

After supper we took turns using the toilet—girls first, and then the boys, and no peeking. Then we washed up at the little sink. We used soap and a towel from one of our knapsacks. I wondered what prisoners did who were locked into a cell without soap or towels.

Chapter Four

It took me long time to settle down to sleep. It was exciting and a little scary to spend a night in a prison. Mostly, though, I kept thinking about what had happened that afternoon. How could we avoid other hoodlums? I tossed and turned on the lumpy mattress. And could we make it to Waldeck before our sisters left? We had already used up three whole days, and we still had a very long way to go. Tomorrow would be Saturday, May 28—four days before June first!

How long, I wondered, could I pretend to the younger kids that I wasn't worried about all these things? We all knew the trip was urgent, but they still thought of Operation Morningstar as a great adventure. The only way it could succeed, it seemed to me, was for them to keep on thinking that way. I yawned and turned over again. Well, at least we had made it this far.

Little did I know what awaited all of us in the morning.

Chapter 5
1945

Saturday, May 28, through Sunday, May 29

"Six o'clock! Everybody up!" The voice startled me out of my sleep. I opened my eyes and remembered that we had just spent the night in Nuremberg prison. Thin shafts of sunlight were filtering through a barred window high on the wall opposite my bunk. Rudy was sprawled on the bunk above me, and below us, on the floor, Volfie lay curled up on his mattress like a shrimp. The girls' mattress lay along the front wall of the cell. Helga was still asleep, but Heidi was sitting upright, listening. "They're bringing breakfast," she whispered.

In a few moments the door panel slid sideways, and a tray full of tin dishes appeared. This time there was a pot of mush, some coarse black bread, and more black coffee.

Once again we ate heartily, not knowing where we would get our next meal.

We had no sooner finished than we heard voices in the passageway and a knock at the door. Larry entered, followed by a guard—a different one from the night before—and another American soldier. They all looked serious.

"We've got a little problem," said Larry, slowly rubbing the back of his neck. "I've been trying to work out a ride for you to Wurzburg."

"Yes?" I asked. Wurzberg, the next big city, was almost halfway to Waldeck.

Larry looked nervously at the other soldier, who spoke up. "You'll need special papers in order to continue traveling," he said, crossing his arms.

"What kind of papers?" I asked. The words almost caught in my throat. We all stood frozen.

"Evidence of sponsorship," said the officer, stroking his chin. "Someone has to be responsible for you."

I explained that we were from a camp in Czechoslovakia and we had no papers. We had fled the Russians. There had been no time for such things.

He shook his head. "We can't just turn you loose in Wurzburg."

I could feel my eyes smarting, and someone was sniffling. "Please, sir," I said, "we've got to find our father!"

He put his hand on my shoulder. "Lots of kids want to find their parents these days. We understand how you feel, but roaming around the countryside is just too dangerous. We can't allow it."

"But what else can we do?" Rudy asked.

The officer looked down at Rudy. "There's a place in Wurzburg where you could go. . . ." The two men looked at each other, and then he continued, "It's run by some Catholic nuns."

"There are lots of other kids there," said Larry, "and they'll take good care of you."

I looked back and forth at each of them, pleading with my eyes. "Please, just let us go on by ourselves. We'll be fine, really we will." I wanted to push the soldiers out of the way and run out of there.

The new officer just shook his head, and in a few minutes we were back in a jeep, this time bouncing along the highway toward Wurzburg. All the time we rode, my mind was racing, trying to figure out what to do.

"Will they make us stay long?" asked Heidi.

"I hope not," I said. There had to be some way out of this situation.

"But what about the papers?" asked Helga. "What'll we do without papers?"

"We don't know, Helga," said Rudy, leaning forward so he could see around me to where Helga sulked in a corner. "We'll figure out a way."

"I wish we'd never left," she said, watching the countryside flying past.

"Don't be stupid, Helga," I snapped. "Just be glad we've gotten this far." But I wasn't feeling glad about anything at that point.

We rode straight through the center of Wurzburg and up a long hill toward a large white mansion. A wooden porch ran along three sides, and a tall chimney stood like a sentinel on the end of the gabled roof.

"Is this where we're going to stay?" asked Volfie, smiling as we drove past the gateposts.

"Yes," said the driver, braking at the front door. "They'll take good care of you."

I didn't want to be taken care of. I wanted to turn and run when we got out of the jeep, but I knew it was no use.

A young woman in an apron answered our knock, ushered us into a drafty entrance hall, and asked us to wait a moment. I smelled food, and the thought of it helped ease the pain of being forced to come here.

The hallway had probably once been elegant, but now the room was bare, and the red brocade wallpaper was faded except where large paintings had once hung. The soldier leaned against a door frame and fidgeted, and the rest of us stood glumly, listening to the sounds of children from behind a door down the hall.

In a few moments, a smiling woman in a black nun's habit came sweeping across the bare wooden floor. Her face was framed with starched white fabric, and tired blue eyes peered out through her wire-rimmed eyeglasses. She held out her hand to the soldier. "I am Mother Frieda," she said. Then she looked us over gravely. "You look like you've come a long way."

The soldier nodded. "They're nice kids," he said. "Their mother's dead, and the father might be too."

"Oh, no," I said quickly. "He's in Witten."

She nodded, but she didn't say anything.

The soldier looked over at me. "Name's Mueller,

right?" He hadn't asked us our first names.

I cleared my throat. "I'm Katrina Mueller, and this is Rudy, Helga, Heidi, and Volfgang. But we can't stay."

Mother Frieda shook hands with each of us and ignored what I had said. "We are just having lunch," she said. "Won't you join us?" She gestured to the American. "You, too."

"Thanks, ma'am, but I have to get back. Think you can take them?" he asked.

The nun straightened her glasses and frowned. "I think so. We just placed four this morning."

I wondered what "placed" meant.

After the soldier left, Mother Frieda led us through a chipped white door into what once might have been a ballroom. Dozens of children were sitting on long wooden benches, eating soup at oilcloth-covered tables. Their chattering stopped when we came in, and dozens of pairs of eyes followed us as we crossed the room.

Mother Frieda moved swiftly past the tables, greeting the children as we trailed behind her. She stopped near the back of the room, where two dark-haired girls sat by themselves. One was about my age. She looked up and flashed a smile at Mother Frieda.

"We have some new friends today," the nun announced cheerfully. The chin of the younger girl barely cleared the top of her soup bowl. Her large blue eyes had dark circles under them.

"These are the Muellers," Mother Frieda told them, gesturing for us to sit down. "You tell each other your first names. I'm going to see that you get something to eat."

I dropped gratefully down onto the bench. To my relief, the children at the other tables started chattering again, and no one seemed to pay much attention to us.

The older girl spoke up. "I'm Greta," she said, and she nodded at the younger girl. "And that's Marta, my little sister." Marta flashed a smile and went on spooning up her soup. Her hair hung limply below her shoulders. I wondered if anyone ever braided it.

We had just told them our names when a stooped man appeared with a tray of steaming soup bowls. He slammed one down in front of each of us, spilling some each time. The soup was watery white with a few lumps of potato, but I couldn't wait to eat it.

The man glanced at us and said, "If they bring any more kids in this place, we're all going to go hungry." He turned and limped off, shaking his head and mumbling.

Greta made a face. "Don't pay any attention to Hans," she said. "He's always grouchy." But I winced, remembering our aunts at the villa.

"Where are you from?" asked Greta, returning to her meal.

"Schwandorf," I said, picking up my spoon. "Well, Witten, really."

"That's where our father is," said Rudy.

"You have a father?" She looked surprised.

"Yes. We all lived in Witten before the war." Then he told her about Mama.

Greta's face clouded. "That's what happened to both of our parents," she said.

"Oh, how awful," I said. I couldn't think of anything

more to say about anything so sad, so I asked her what I dreaded knowing. "Is this an orphanage?"

Greta set down her spoon. "It is now," she said. "It used to be a rich man's house, but he died, so they use it for us."

"Us?"

"War orphans," said Greta, passing a plate of bread. "That's what we all are."

"Well, we're not!" said Rudy, straightening up. "We have a father."

"But where is he?"

"In Witten."

Greta just looked at him and went on eating.

Marta pushed back her bowl. "We get good food here," she said. "You'll like it."

"Oh, but we're not—" I stopped. Better not to say anything more at this point.

Mother Frieda asked me a lot of questions later— where we had come from and how we had gotten this far. She kept shaking her head all the time I was talking. Then she took us to the attic rooms where we would stay, boys in one room, girls in another. The rooms were bare compared to Frau Schmidt's cozy bedrooms, and the mattresses on the cots didn't look much thicker than the blankets that were spread over them. But at least it was a place to sleep for that night.

After Mother Frieda had gone downstairs, we all gathered in one of the rooms and shut the door.

"How long can we stay at this place?" asked Volfie anxiously. He tugged at my sleeve as he spoke.

Helga answered him. "We're not staying. Why should we?"

"It's not so bad," he replied, twisting a lock of his hair.

"It would be if you had to stay here forever, dummy," said Helga. Volfie was quiet after that.

"Maybe we could sneak out during the night," said Rudy.

"Someone might hear us," I said, "and then we'd be in big trouble." I walked over to the window. "Besides, we don't know anything about this town—where to go, I mean."

"I'd be scared to go out there in the dark," said Heidi.

"Me, too," said Helga.

I turned around and faced the others. "We're just going to have to leave sometime tomorrow, first chance we get. Don't worry; I'll think of some way. And don't tell anyone," I cautioned them. Everyone nodded.

We went outside afterward, and children were all over the yard. Some were playing tag, but others were playing jump rope or just standing around in small groups. That's when I noticed how many were barefoot. At least we Muellers still had shoes. *That's something to be grateful for,* I thought.

Except for Greta, most of the girls were younger than I, so I hung around her and helped push the little kids on the swings.

"Where are you from?" I asked her, pushing a swing where a little girl sat as I talked.

"Berlin," she said. "At least, that's where my mother and I were staying when the bomb hit. My father was in the army."

"Did he get killed fighting?"

"No, he was on leave. He had just come home when it happened." She pushed harder.

The little boy on the swing turned his head and called back to her, "Higher, Greta!"

"Stick your legs out!" she said. "Now, tuck them under!" She gave him another hard push.

"How long have you been here?" I asked, helping the little girl down from the swing.

"About four months," she replied. She looked away, but when she looked back her eyes were full of tears. "You get used to it," she added.

I didn't answer her.

The nuns helped us wash our clothes that night. We hung them in the basement so there would be no wash on the line the next day, which was Sunday. Sunday was a day of rest here, just as it had been at the parsonage in Witten.

The next morning we were rested and scrubbed, and wore outsized clothing that the nuns had lent us until our own were dry. They even found some extra clothes for Rudy to replace what had been stolen.

We joined the rest of the children as they filed into the makeshift chapel for mass. It was dark in the chapel—darker, at least, than it used to be in our Lutheran church. Up front a large cross stood poised atop a wooden pedestal. Glued onto it was an almost naked and very dead-looking Jesus. Above the crucifix—that's what Papa called Catholic crosses—was a painting of Jesus. He wore a blue robe over a white one, and on the left side of his chest was a large red heart. It looked real, and drops of blood were painted below it. I kept looking at it and wondering what Papa would think if he could see us in that chapel, Lutherans that we were.

I sneaked a glance over at Volfie. He was swinging his legs and watching everything closely. Heidi and Helga sat giggling with two other girls about their ages. They were all dressed in the same white pinafores. Rudy sat next to me, and he just stared straight ahead. You could never be sure what Rudy was thinking.

A priest stood by the altar saying the mass. He spoke in Latin, so I couldn't understand it, but some of it reminded me of our Lutheran service.

When it was time for prayer, the children dropped to their knees on the bare floor and started mumbling. I waited, and then I knelt down too. Mostly I thought about how hard the floor was. Besides, I wasn't sure about prayer—or God—anymore. Not since the bombers had come to Witten . . .

By the time mass was over, I was more determined than ever that we would leave this place as quickly as possible. This was definitely not going to be home for the Muellers. Then at about four o'clock that afternoon, everything came crashing down around me.

Chapter 6

1945

Sunday, May 29, through
Tuesday, May 31

Mother Frieda had asked Rudy and me to come into her office. Two other nuns were sitting alongside her neatly arranged desk. One of them, Sister Genevieve, had been at the chapel service. The other was introduced as Sister Anna. They were very solemn, and they watched us intently as Mother Frieda talked. Behind them, huge raindrops kept slamming against a pair of partly draped windows and chasing each other down the long glass panels.

Mother Frieda told us she understood completely how important it seemed to us to be on our way again. "Seemed," she said. It didn't just *seem* important. It was the most important thing in the world! I shifted uncomfortably in my chair.

"You know, most of the children here have come just as you did, trying to find lost relatives." She shook her head. "Sadly, though, it will take many months for all those families to be reunited. In the meantime . . ."

I could feel my heart pounding. "But, Mother Frieda, we can't wait that long!" I said.

Rudy spoke up. "Our sisters are leaving in three more days! We have to get to them, or we may never find our father!"

"He might go with them!" I added, almost shrilly. The truth of the matter was that we knew precious little about their plans, but we clung to any shred of news after months of not knowing whether they were even alive.

Mother Frieda peered at us over her glasses and shook her head again. "I understand how painful this is, but you will never make it out there by yourselves." She leaned forward. "You simply don't realize the terrible things that have happened, especially to young girls—just like you, Katrina."

I sat wringing my hands. "Please, Mother Frieda, we *have* to go."

"We have a map," said Rudy eagerly, "and people will help us. We've already had several rides."

She looked at him. "You were lucky," she said. Then she looked back at me. "Believe me, if I thought it were safe, I would be the first to send you on your way. But I cannot." At that she rose to leave. She turned to the other nuns and whispered something, but I heard it: "Watch them closely."

Wherever we went that evening, I could feel the nuns' eyes on us. At supper, Rudy muttered, "I wish we could eat in our rooms. I feel like a criminal or something."

Helga shoved her spoon around in her cornmeal mush. "When we were in the prison, we were free," she said. "Now look at us! We're prisoners!"

"We'll never get out, either," said Rudy. "They're watching every move we make!"

They were watching us, all right. Sister Genevieve stood with her arms crossed, talking with Sister Anna. Every once in a while they glanced at us as if they were afraid we'd disappear into thin air.

"I don't know what we can do, Rudy," I said. A tight knot had formed in my stomach, and my head was splitting. "I've got to get out of here for a while." I told the nuns I had to go to the bathroom and left the dining room.

Once out of sight, I rushed through the empty front hallway and up the broad staircase. I was surprised to see Greta when I reached the top. "What's wrong?" she asked.

"Everything," I said. Greta followed me up to the attic bedroom.

After closing the door, I told her how Mother Frieda refused to let us leave. "The nuns are watching us all the time!" I said. "I feel like an animal trapped in a cage."

Greta put her arms around me for a long moment, and then she stood back and took my hands in hers. "They have good reasons for keeping you here, you know," she said. Her dark eyes looked grave.

I shook my head and sank down on one of the cots. Greta joined me. "Traveling alone is dangerous these days," she said.

"But we've been fine so far," I insisted, "and we

have to get to Waldeck as soon as possible."

Greta sat quietly for a minute. Then her face brightened. "I've got it!" she exclaimed. "Morning prayers!"

"What?"

"When the bell rings at ten tomorrow morning, all the nuns will go into the chapel for prayer."

I didn't understand.

"Get everybody ready as soon as breakfast is over. Hide your knapsacks in the parlor off the front hall. After the nuns go into the chapel, grab the packs and run."

"But what if they don't all go in?"

"They always do."

"But how . . ."

"Do you want to go or don't you? I'll watch and give you a signal."

Someone banged on the door. We jumped up, and Greta hid behind the door as I opened it. It was Sister Genevieve.

"Are you all right?" she asked.

I stepped forward into the doorway. "Yes," I said, pretending to wipe my eyes. "I had to get a handkerchief from my knapsack."

The nun smiled back and slipped an arm across my shoulders as we headed for the stairs.

"Everybody here is homesick at times," she said. "Don't worry. You'll feel better as the days go by." She let me go first down the steps.

"I guess so," I said. I was glad she couldn't see me smile.

That evening Sister Genevieve helped me take down

our dry clothes from the basement clothesline. I carried them upstairs, and we each folded our own.

"Put these on in the morning, so you'll be ready to leave," I whispered to my sisters and brothers. "And have your knapsacks packed and ready to go." Then I told them what Greta and I had planned—how we could escape while the nuns were in the chapel.

"Not while they're praying!" said Heidi, knitting her eyebrows together. "That doesn't seem right."

"Oh, for heaven's sake, Heidi," said Helga, rolling her eyes. "Be practical for once in your life!"

"It's our only chance," I said. "Then we might still make it in time. That is, if nothing else stops us."

The next morning, as the nuns knelt in the chapel— probably asking for God's help in caring for all their children—five of those children, clutching their knapsacks, slipped out the door of the orphanage. Desperate, I found myself praying all the way down the long, winding driveway. "Please, God, don't let them stop us!"

Someone saw us, though. Hans came limping along just as we darted through the gateway. I almost bumped into him.

"Watch where you're going!" he snarled. We kept running, not daring to look back. When I finally peeked, he was still standing on the sidewalk, scratching his head.

"What if he tells Mother Frieda?" asked Helga, catching up with me.

"He's probably glad to see us leave," I replied, breathless.

"Yeah," she said. "Five less mouths to feed."

We divided into two groups to be less noticeable. Rudy stayed ahead with Volfie, and the girls and I followed half a block behind. We stayed on the side streets until we left Wurzburg, and then we hiked together through the fields so we wouldn't be seen on the highway.

The rain we'd had the day before had stopped, and a brisk wind had dried up most of the puddles. Even so, the sky was still cloudy, and I felt gloomy inside, afraid we'd be spotted and returned to the orphanage. On an impulse, I pulled one of my braids around and loosened the tie, letting my hair fall down my back.

"You look different that way," said Heidi.

"I know," I said, loosening the other braid. "I want to look different." I looked over at her and Helga. "And I think you'd better, too." So Heidi and Helga soon trudged along with their blond hair flying out like streamers behind them.

It was midafternoon before we came to a small town. We hadn't eaten since breakfast, so the girls and I headed for a corner market while Rudy and Volfie waited in the shadows across the street.

The shop smelled of sawdust and pickles. We chose some cheese and pumpernickel bread, and I was digging into my pack for the money when two American army officers came in. They watched as I placed three crumpled marks into the shopkeeper's hand, and then one of them asked, "Been doing some traveling?"

My heart almost stopped. "A little," I said, smiling and smoothing my hair back nervously. I was grateful we had at least started out that morning in clean clothes.

" Is anyone else with you?" asked the officer,

glancing toward the shop window.

I shook my head and eased past him. "Excuse me, sir," I mumbled. "Our mother needs these groceries." Helga and Heidi followed me with their eyes down.

I heard the shopkeeper's voice as I opened the door. "Looking for anyone in particular?" he asked the soldier. I paused.

"Yes. We just received word that five children ran off from an orphanage back in . . ."

I yanked the door shut, and the three of us tore down the street and around a corner. The boys followed at a distance, and we never stopped running until we reached a bridge near the edge of town. One by one, we ducked underneath and crouched there like frightened rabbits. We had to sit on a slanting concrete slab, but at least we were out of sight. We decided to stay until nightfall, when it would be safer to start out.

By the time it got dark, however, it was raining again. We huddled together, shivering in the blackness and listening as raindrops pelted the ground nearby and the bridge overhead.

"I'm getting wet," said Volfie.

I fumbled around in my knapsack, wishing like anything I had the flashlight. "Here," I said, handing him our towel. "Wrap up in this. And come over here next to me where it's drier."

Volfie squirmed around for a few moments, adjusting the towel and squeezing himself between Rudy and me. After a while he sighed and asked in a sleepy voice, "How long do we have to stay here?"

"Until the rain stops," I said. "Then we'll start out again."

"In the dark?" asked Volfie. I felt him tense up.

I patted him. "Just so we can get farther away," I said.

Heidi started sniffling on the other side of me.

"You okay?" I asked.

She leaned against me. "Just sad," she said. I slipped my arm around her. "I want to go home," she said.

"I know." I bit my lip and hugged her, grateful that she couldn't read my thoughts.

After a while everyone seemed to be asleep. With both Volfie and Heidi leaning against me, I couldn't move for fear of waking them. The day's events kept running through my mind like a movie—fleeing from the orphanage, the soldier in the market, more running, and now scrunched together under this bridge. How long would we have to keep hiding? What might happen to us if we had to travel only at night? We'd never be able to get any more rides. *Dear God,* I found myself praying, *please help us. . . .* I felt exhausted and confused.

Eventually, I slept. I don't know how long it was, but when we all woke up, the rain had stopped. Faint pink clouds stretched across the eastern horizon, but overhead the sky was still a solid dark blue.

We hurried to get out of the town before sunrise. After that we planned to cross the fields again as we headed north.

"How much farther?" asked Volfie, slipping his hand into Rudy's.

Chapter Six

"A good ways yet," said Rudy, looking down at him. "But we'll make it somehow."

I wondered if he believed it. The distance we still had to cover made my stomach tighten whenever I thought of it. But for now at least we felt safe, traveling while no one was up. As the sky lightened, even the gray stucco houses hugging the sidewalks looked asleep, with their window shades pulled down like closed eyelids.

Hiking over fields was harder than on the road, but at least we could stay together. And purple clover and yellow buttercups nodding in the breeze made the walk almost pleasant.

In the midafternoon, just as we had reached a ridge on the far edge of the next town, we saw it: a railroad train sitting on the tracks alongside an old stone station. Hardly any trains were running anywhere in Germany, but here was a locomotive belching out big puffs of smoke, and it was pointed north.

Chapter 1

1945

Tuesday, May 31, through Wednesday, June 1

Dozens of men were perched on the long line of box-cars that stretched behind the locomotive. "Why are they up there?" asked Volfie, shading his eyes.

"Probably too crowded inside," said Rudy.

I strained to see. The men looked like swarming ants from where I stood. "Maybe they're returning troops," I said.

"Katrina," Rudy said suddenly, "get out the map."

We checked our penciled route up to Giessen, the next large city on our way. Near the road we intended to follow, train tracks led directly northward to Giessen.

"This might be our chance," said Rudy.

"Let's try to catch it," I said, stuffing the map back

into my knapsack. I knew we had to hurry.

We started running as fast as our legs would carry us. If we could catch the train, we could save hours and hours of walking! The road was littered with gravel, and halfway there Volfie suddenly tripped and fell. I swooped down and pulled him to his feet. We continued running, with me holding tightly to his hand.

As we came closer, I could see the boxcar riders better. They were German solders all right. And they were cheering and waving—at us! "Wait!" we called, waving furiously as we raced along.

Just then, the train did what I most feared; it began to move.

"Stop!" we cried. "Stop!" But the train kept moving, gaining speed as it rolled along the tracks. I kept thinking we were crazy to run after a train, but I couldn't bear the thought of missing it. "Stop!" we yelled at the top of our lungs.

Suddenly there was a loud hiss of steam. To our astonishment, the train was braking! The cars started slowing down, and in a few moments they had stopped completely. The soldiers cheered, and two of them leaned down from the coal car. "Here!" they shouted. "Take our hands."

Within moments, they managed to pull us, one at a time, up the outside ladder and down into the car. I held my breath until all five of us had made it. Panting and laughing, we picked our way over the coal that half-filled the inside.

The train lurched and started up again, throwing us down onto the hard, grimy lumps. We pulled ourselves back up, breathless and hardly believing that we had actually caught the train. I turned to the soldiers. "Why did it stop?" I asked, still panting.

"Everyone saw you and yelled to the engineer," said one, as if stopping trains were commonplace.

"You *are* going toward Giessen, aren't you?" I asked.

"Right," said the other soldier. "First train in weeks."

The soldiers led Rudy and Volfie up to a ledge near the top so they could see out. The girls and I stayed below, grateful to catch our breath at last.

Heidi nudged me and nodded toward the soldiers. "More angels, Trina," she said.

I smiled at her. Heidi seemed convinced that we were getting some sort of heavenly help along the way. *Well, no matter,* I thought. *As long as it makes it easier for her.* But I wondered what Mama and Papa would have said if they could have seen us at that moment: black dust all over ourselves and grinning from ear to ear as we sat on a pile of coal, headed for an unknown city.

After a while we joined the others on the ledge. Up there, with the wind whipping around our heads, we could see the countryside and the soldiers sprawled across the boxcar roofs. Their gray-green uniforms were soiled and ragged.

Helga leaned toward me so that I could hear her over the wind and the chugging of the locomotive. "Trina," she yelled. "Some of these soldiers aren't much older than Rudy!"

"They ran out of men toward the end, Helga," I replied. I shuddered, thinking how even Rudy might have had to serve, had the war continued. And if he had refused . . . I shuddered again, remembering how Mama's cousin Dietrich had been dragged off to prison for opposing Hitler. He and so many others. We never knew what became of them.

The train moved slowly through the lush countryside. Farmers were plowing up the damage done during the fighting. Broad tire tracks crisscrossed the fields not yet plowed, and here and there an abandoned, battered tank stood as a silent reminder of the war so recently ended.

In a little while the girls and I jumped back down on the coal. The taller of the soldiers joined us and let us sit on his duffel bag. "It's a bit more comfortable than coal," he said, smiling at us. We sat down gratefully. The soldier squatted in front of us. His uniform was tattered, but his smile was warm. "By the way, name's Kriner," he said, holding out his hand. "Fritz Kriner. What's yours, and where do you come from?"

We told him our story, and he told us his. He and Dieter Braun, the other soldier, were childhood friends. They were returning to Hamburg in northern Germany after serving in Hitler's army for more than five years.

"I'm so sick of war," said Fritz, shaking his head. "I don't even care that we lost." He pushed his steel-rimmed glasses back up on his nose. "I just want to go home as fast as I can."

I nodded, wondering where home was for me at that point. The parsonage was gone. What kind of a house would Papa be living in? Papa. Hopefully, it wouldn't be long. . . .

Suddenly Fritz said to me, "You know, this train

wasn't expected to run until next month. It really is a godsend."

"What did you say?"

He raised his voice. "This train—it's a godsend!" He looked to see if I understood. "We hadn't expected it."

I smiled and yelled back, "You're right. It's wonderful to be traveling so fast." *Godsend. Interesting word,* I thought. Never thought much about it before.

Heidi shifted on the duffel bag and leaned against me. In a few moments her eyes closed, and she fell fast asleep, lulled by the motion of the train.

Later, Dieter and the boys jumped down and settled on Dieter's bag. Volfie leaned against Rudy, and soon he too was asleep. The sky overhead slowly turned to gray and then to black. Soon the train would be stopping, for no one could travel in Germany at night anymore.

Helga shifted her position on the bag. "I'm hungry," she said. "I hope we can eat soon."

I slipped my arm around her. "I know," I said. We had eaten the last of our bread and cheese that morning and had had nothing since then. "We'll eat as soon as we can," I added. We still had a couple of marks left, but I had no idea if we would find anyplace open by the time we arrived. Nor did we know, for that matter, where we might sleep that night.

When we pulled into the heavily damaged station at Giessen, Red Cross workers were there in the midst of the rubble, helping soldiers off the train and wheeling in steaming pots of soup.

Fritz approached one of the workers. "Could these

children have some supper, too? They've come a long way, and they're very hungry."

The Red Cross worker readily agreed. She had us all sit down on our knapsacks right there on the platform and brought us each a brimming bowlful of hot, sweet soup. It was made with cream of wheat and milk—real milk! It had been months since we'd had any, and we could scarcely believe our eyes. No meal ever tasted so good.

As we were finishing up, a woman about Mama's age came by. "I could tell by the way you were eating your soup," she said, "that you were very hungry."

We nodded and watched her solemnly.

The woman continued, "Before long you will be hungry again, so take this with you." She handed me a can of stew. I turned it over in my hand, marveling at the sight of a real can of stew with *meat* in it. When I looked up to thank her, she had disappeared into the darkness of the bombed-out station.

"Look, Rudy," I said, handing my brother the precious can.

Rudy stared at it in amazement. "Put it in your knapsack quick, and don't lose it!"

"Don't worry," I said, tucking it inside. "It's like gold."

"Better than gold if we get hungry enough," said Rudy.

Heidi just watched and smiled. I knew what she was thinking.

Fritz and Dieter went off to see about a place to spend the night. While they were gone, we found public toilets and took turns with our soap and towel. As I returned them to my knapsack, Volfie said, "The soap is getting smaller and smaller."

I was afraid it might disappear completely before we reached Waldeck. But I all I said was, "I wish we could change our clothes. These are so sooty!"

"We'll just get sooty again tomorrow," he replied. Dirt never bothered nine-year-old boys.

When the soldiers came back, they told us that the Red Cross had fixed a room for returning servicemen right there in the station. "You can sleep here too," said Fritz.

"There's no electricity," said Dieter, "but I've got a flashlight." I thought again about the hoodlums who had taken ours in Herrsbruck.

We followed Dieter's circle of light into the darkened room. Snoring soldiers were sprawled everywhere. We groped our way past several rows of wooden benches until we finally found an empty one. We took turns sleeping on it, and, thanks to the Red Cross, we had warm blankets for both the bench and the floor.

By daylight, as we returned to the concourse, we saw that one whole end of the station was boarded up, and blue sky showed through a gaping hole in the ceiling. At least it wasn't raining!

The Red Cross had porridge ready, so soon we were well-filled and eager to leave. Today was June 1. Another train ride, another walk, and we would be in Waldeck! We hugged the workers and thanked them for their kindness.

"Be careful," said one, hugging me in return.

"We will be," I said. But I wasn't sure what "careful"

was anymore. It seemed like nothing we had done lately was very careful. *If we had been careful,* I thought, *we would probably have stayed in Schwandorf.* Besides, we were almost at the end of our journey.

As it turned out, we stood around on the station platform most of the morning, waiting for the train to start up.

"We'll never make it now," said Rudy.

"Maybe we can," I said. "We can cover a lot of ground once we get started."

Finally the engineer fired up the huge, black locomotive and told us that we could get on board. Dieter had been talking with someone farther down the platform. He came back looking troubled. "Bad news," he said. "I just heard that this train will take us only about sixty more kilometers." Less than an hour's ride.

Chapter 5
1945

Wednesday Morning

Sixty more kilometers! My stomach tightened. "We'll never make it to Waldeck today," I muttered to Rudy, as we moved toward the nearest freight car.

"Not with this short a ride," he agreed.

Fritz and Dieter hopped up into the doorway and helped the rest of us into the crowded car. It smelled like manure, and the floor was covered with straw. "Be careful where you step," said Fritz.

Soon the sliding door slammed shut. We grabbed onto the slats along the side of the car as we lurched backward and the train started rolling along the tracks.

From the thin shafts of light that sifted between the slats, we could see that the straw was too dirty to sit on. Instead, we all stood together in a corner. I was glad for the semi-darkness. It hid my obvious concern. I was more worried than ever, and it was so important to appear calm.

"We'll be in Waldeck tonight, won't we?" asked Volfie from somewhere down between Rudy and me.

Rudy and I glanced at each other, and then I looked at my little brother. I answered slowly, trying to accept the words myself. "No, Volfie. We're not going to make it."

Helga heard us. "But we have to!"

"Well, we can't," I snapped. Then I tossed my head. "We'll just have to keep going and hope they haven't left yet, that's all."

"It'll be too late," Helga shot back. Then she added, "I knew this would happen."

"Well, it wasn't my fault!"

Rudy spoke up. "But what if they've already left by the time we get there?"

"That's the chance we'll have to take, I guess."

Heidi interrupted, "Maybe Aunt Brigette never said it was June first. Maybe she said the first week in June!"

Always the optimist, I thought. I looked away. I was tired of talking about it—tired of trying to be Mama. *If I was at home,* I thought, *I could run up to my room and slam the door.*

"Look," said Fritz gently, "you did everything you possibly could to get up there on time, didn't you?"

I nodded soberly.

"And none of you could walk sixty kilometers in a day, so this is still a help, right?"

I had to agree.

Much to our relief, Fritz and Dieter told us they would stay with us until the next day. After that they had to head north to Hamburg. Waldeck was to the northwest.

Everything seemed to brighten once I knew the soldiers would be around a little longer. They could be in charge instead of me. *And who knows,* I thought, *maybe Heidi is right about it being the first week, not June first.* Anyway, we would keep going.

Suddenly the train slowed down and came to a halt. Through the slats we saw a small railway station and some men talking on the platform. Three were American soldiers. We stood waiting, wondering what was going on, when suddenly the door slid sideways, letting in a flood of sunlight.

"Everybody out!" someone called from the platform.

"Why?" asked a soldier near the door. "We just got started."

"There's a delay. Might as well stretch your legs."

I looked around cautiously as I jumped down onto the platform. Would the American soldiers start asking questions? I started to head in the opposite direction, but to my relief they moved on down the platform and seemed busy with other things.

It did feel good to walk around. We didn't dare go very far off, though, except to use the toilets in the station.

"We're lucky," said Helga, as we stood washing our hands at the small, grimy sink. "We didn't have to wait in line with all those soldiers."

"It pays to be a girl," said Heidi, standing on her tiptoes and smiling at her reflection in the cracked mirror over the sink.

I looked into the mirror too. It was the first time I'd seen myself since I'd left the bedroom at Frau Schmidt's.

My face was pale and thin, and my hair, loosened from the braids, was straggly and dirty. How I wished I could wash it.

The others were lined up for the men's room when we came back out into the station. Volfie looked cross, and I gladly kept my distance. Let Rudy be the one to try to reason with him for a change.

There were no Red Cross workers at this little station and no place to buy anything for lunch. But we were on the outskirts of a little town, and I wondered if there might be a store nearby.

Rudy must have read my thoughts. "I'm starved," he said, when he came back outside. "Let me go see if I can find some food."

In spite of my hunger, I shook my head. "No, you'd better not," I said. "The train could leave."

"I'll hear it start up," he said. "Give me some money. Please! I'm so hungry! I promise I'll be right back."

I finally dug into my knapsack and brought out our last two marks. "This is all we have left," I told Rudy, handing him the money. "Be careful with it."

"I will." He turned and ran up the street toward the little village. I felt a lump in my throat as I watched him disappear.

"What if he doesn't come back in time?" asked Heidi.

"He will. He's got to," I said, biting my lip. I watched the street nervously as the minutes passed.

Volfie started to whine. "I'm hungry," he said. "Why doesn't Rudy come back?"

Chapter Eight

"He'll be here any minute," I said, checking the street again.

A loud blast of steam burst from the engine, and the conductor yelled, "All aboard!"

I strained to look for Rudy. No sign of him anywhere. All the soldiers except Fritz and Dieter were boarding the train.

"What shall we do?" asked Helga, pressing her hands against her cheeks.

"Wait for him, of course!"

"But we'll miss the train!"

I didn't answer. I shielded my eyes from the sun, straining to catch a glimpse of my brother. Where in the world was Rudy? *I should never have let him go,* I thought, much as we needed food. All I had left in my knapsack was the can of stew and a little sugar and flour.

The station master came up. "Train's going to leave without you if you don't get back on," he said.

Fritz said, "Their brother had to go to get some food."

The man turned to leave. "We can't wait," he said. "We're already behind schedule."

I looked up at Fritz. "You two go ahead," I said.

Fritz shook his head. "We're not going to leave you alone." He started to say something to the station master, when all of a sudden Rudy appeared in the distance, tearing down the street toward us. In a few moments he stood, breathless, in front of me, a bulging parcel under his arm.

"I'm sorry," he said, as Dieter pulled us back up into the car.

This time everyone was sitting down. Either the floor was cleaner in this car, or they were too tired to care. We quickly joined them.

With the door shut and the train clickity-clacking along, Rudy apologized to me again. "I couldn't find a store that was open. Finally I found someone who knew where to get bread." He set his parcel down in front of us and glanced up at me. "It took all the money," he said.

I nodded soberly. He'd bought the bread on the black market, I was sure of it. That's the only way he could have found some and paid so much money for it. We both had dealt in the black market back in Schwandorf. I used to take cigarettes the American soldiers gave me for washing their clothes. A dealer in town would buy them—three marks a pack. That's how we'd saved the money for the trip.

Rudy lifted a long loaf of pumpernickel from the crinkly brown paper. We huddled around the brown bread as if it were a rare treasure, which indeed it was.

I gave Rudy a quick hug. "This is wonderful—just what we need," I said. "And don't forget, we still have our can of stew for tonight." I closed my eyes briefly and thought, *We'll make it through today!* Gratefully, I started breaking the bread into big chunks—seven of them. But when I handed one to Fritz, he shook his head.

"We can't take your bread."

"Don't be silly! Of course you can!" I turned to Dieter. "Here, have some."

Dieter looked over at Fritz, and then he said, "No, you and the children eat it."

"All right, then," I announced, "we'll share it with

everyone in the car." And with that I started breaking the bread into smaller pieces. Heidi joined me, and soon we had a pile large enough for everyone, including Fritz and Dieter.

While we were breaking the bread, a few of the soldiers started rummaging in their duffel bags. Out came wedges of cheese, several ration packs of crackers, and even a few salted fish—all hoarded away out of fear of starvation. Put together, we had enough so that everyone could eat. Even Fritz and Dieter.

A strange quiet settled on us as we shared that meal. I looked around at all the men's faces—tired, dirty, and bearded, but glowing at the same time. The quiet continued for a long while even after we were finished.

Someone on the other side of the car started singing a German folk song, and soon everyone was singing along with him. We sang other songs, too. The last one was melancholy, about childhood and home. I couldn't even finish the first verse.

Outside it had started to rain, and water was coming in along our side of the car. We moved away from the slats, but we had barely gotten resettled when the train slowed down and came to a stop.

Fritz looked out. "This must be it," he said.

That was indeed as far as the train went that day. Within minutes we were following Fritz and Dieter through the pouring rain, trying to find shelter in a small, unknown town.

Wednesday Afternoon

The water running across the sidewalks leaked into my shoes, making my toes squish with every step. By the time we found a doorway to crowd under, all of us were soaked. We stood and waited for the downpour to let up, watching the sheets of rain hammer across the cobblestones and swirl down the gutters.

After a while I asked Fritz, "What time do you suppose it is?"

"Must be after four o'clock by now. When the rain lets up I think we'd better try to find the town hall. Someone there might be able to help us find a place to stay tonight."

For a long while the street was deserted, but finally a man came hustling along under a large, black umbrella, hunkered down against the wind and the rain.

Fritz ran over to him. "Where can we find the town hall?" he yelled.

"Up there!" cried the man, pointing.

We waited a few more minutes until the rain had almost stopped, and then we all dashed down the street to the building the man had shown us. Dieter yanked on the front door, and we darted inside, out of breath and dripping wet.

The entrance hall was chilly and smelled musty. There were several doors, but only one was open. Fritz crossed over and stuck his head into it. He brought it out again. "No one in there," he said. Then he called out, "Anybody here?"

A short, bald man with tiny, round glasses opened one of the other doors. "Can I help you?" he asked.

"Yes, please," said Fritz, holding out his hand. "My name's Kriner, and we need some help."

The man shook Fritz's hand. "I'm Wilhelm Koontz," he said. "Town constable." He looked us over. "Got caught in the cloudburst, did you?"

"We sure did," said Fritz. "Sorry we're so wet."

We must have looked wretched. Our hair was plastered to our heads, and our clothes stuck to us. I stood holding onto my elbows and shivering.

Herr Koontz called to a younger man who had come out and stood gaping at us. "Hans," he said, "get some clean rags so they can dry off." He turned back to us. "Haven't seen it rain like this in months. A good thing, too. We're going to need a good harvest this year. . . ."

As we squeezed out our clothes, Fritz told Herr

Koontz where we were headed and that we needed a place for the night.

"We've had a lot of you people lately," said the man. "We try to help when we can. It isn't always possible." He shook his head. "Sometimes there just isn't anything."

I stood rubbing Volfie's head with one of the rags, afraid of what the man might say next. What would we do if there were no place to go, with all this rain coming down?

Herr Koontz stood rubbing his chin. "Some folks just left a deserted house up the street," he said. "They were only there a couple of nights."

I looked up and held my breath.

"Not much of a place, but it's better than sleeping outdoors. Hasn't been lived in in years. I've got a key, and you're welcome to stay if it's just for one night." He rummaged through a drawer and pulled out a brass key on a dirty string.

We followed Herr Koontz down the street toward the house. The rain had stopped, but we still had to skirt the puddles that clung to the sidewalks. A late afternoon sun was trying to shine through the remaining clouds.

"There's a little stove in the house to take the chill off the air," he said, as I traipsed along next to him, "that is, if you can find any wood. . . . And there used to be some furniture. Don't know exactly what's left in there anymore."

The house sat on the far edge of town alongside a meadow. The roof sagged in the middle, and the door creaked open on one hinge, but inside it was dry and almost cozy after the rain. There were only two rooms: a tiny kitchen in the back and a larger room with a small, rusty woodstove. The gas stove in the kitchen didn't work, and the sink had no water in the pipes. The bathroom was a privy in the backyard.

A bare mattress on a rusty bedspring sat along one side of the main room, and a worn couch faced it. A pile of straw filled one of the corners. Near the stove were a rickety table and three wobbly chairs, and, best of all, a small stack of wood for a fire.

"This will be fine," I said to Herr Koontz. It was dry and safe for sleeping. That was the important thing.

"We really appreciate this," said Fritz.

"It's yours until tomorrow," he replied. "Just be sure to lock up when you leave, and bring the key back to me." And with that he left.

Helga and Heidi quickly claimed the bed as their private territory. "Can we sleep here tonight?" asked Helga.

"We're not making any decisions until we all get into dry clothes," I said. I was surprised that I could sound a little bit like Mama.

By ones and twos we went into the kitchen and changed. Thanks to the orphanage, each of us had some clean clothes. It felt good to be dry, too.

After he changed, Fritz opened the door of the stove and began to start a fire. "We're lucky there was wood in here," he said. "Any from outside would be too wet to burn."

In a few minutes, flames were leaping inside the stove, casting dancing shadows on the wall across the room. I took our wet things and draped them over the chairs, hoping they might dry a little once the room warmed up.

Chapter Nine

Dieter produced a deck of cards from his pack and knelt down on the floor in the center of the room. He counted out twenty-one cards, spread them open like a fan, and had Volfie choose one. "Don't tell me what it is," cautioned Dieter, sitting back on his heels.

Volfie grinned, hiding the card behind his back.

"Now put it back in the deck," said Dieter, hiding his eyes.

When the card was safely tucked in between the others, the soldier slapped all of them, one by one, face up on the floor in three neat rows. The rest of us moved over to watch.

"Which row is it in?" asked Dieter.

"The middle one," said Volfie, crossing his arms.

Dieter slid each row closed and stacked the cards together, putting the middle row in the center. Then he laid them out again. "Now which row?" he asked Volfie.

"The first one," said Volfie, looking up at me and grinning.

Dieter closed up the rows, stacked them, and laid them out again. "Now which row?" he asked.

"This one," said Volfie, pointing.

Dieter closed up the cards and started counting them out: slap, slap, slap. He stopped at the jack of spades and held it up. "Your card!" he announced.

Volfie gasped. "How did you do that?"

"Magic!" said Dieter, winking at Fritz.

"Teach me how!" said Helga.

"Me, too!" chanted Volfie and Heidi together.

Knowing they would all be busy for a while, I

picked up a wooden bucket I'd found in the kitchen. "I'm going out to find some water," I said.

"Want me to go with you?" asked Fritz.

I declined his offer, glad to get off by myself for a change.

"Be careful," he replied.

I tossed my head and smiled. "Don't worry."

I walked along toward the center of the town, swinging the bucket as I went. *By this time tomorrow,* I thought, *we may be in Waldeck!* Just thinking about it put a spring into my step.

As I crossed the street, someone came up alongside me. "Look for water?" It was an American soldier with light curly hair and a broad smile.

I smiled back. "There should be a pump up there," I said, nodding toward the center of town.

"I know where. I show you, okay?" he asked.

"Thanks!" I said.

The soldier tried hard to talk with me. His German was very broken, and we laughed as I corrected his pronunciation. He reminded me of the soldiers back at the villa in Schwandorf. I smoothed my hair back, wishing I could have washed it.

We walked along for a couple of blocks. It looked as if this town had not been bombed—no ugly shell holes and no rubble in the yards. The houses were mostly old and needed paint, but at least they all had glass in their windows.

Suddenly the soldier said, "Down here." He pointed to a street off to our left.

Chapter Nine

"Good!" I said, following him gratefully. A shorter walk would help when I had to return with a heavy, filled bucket.

The street led sharply downhill, and it quickly became narrow and dark. The side we were on was bordered by an abandoned brick warehouse, and the buildings across the street were boarded up. I wondered how much farther the pump would be.

"Almost there," said the soldier, leading me into an alleyway next to the warehouse. I looked around for the pump. It was even darker in there, and there was no pump—nothing but brick walls and cobblestones. I stopped walking, and he turned to me. "You pretty," he said, smiling, but something in his eyes had changed.

"Where's the pump?" I demanded.

Chapter 10

1945

Wednesday Evening

The soldier moved closer and tried to stroke my hair. "No," I said, brushing away his arm. He yanked me toward him. "Get away!" I shouted, moving back. I turned to run.

He overtook me and spun me around, pulling me toward him.

"No!" I shouted, swinging my arm. The bucket in my hand hit him squarely on the forehead. He bent forward, holding his head.

"You little . . ."

I tore back up the hill, heading for the cottage. He started after me. Thoughts swirled in my head as I ran. The woman on the truck: *"It's dangerous to travel alone!"* Dangerous! So that's what she meant! My heart was pounding furiously, and I was almost out of breath.

I glanced back and saw that he was gaining on me.

By then I reached the top of the hill, and up ahead someone was coming in our direction. The soldier fell back. The next time I looked, he was gone, but I kept running anyway.

I was exhausted when I arrived back at the cottage. Everyone gathered around me. "What happened?" they wanted to know. I burst into tears and told them haltingly.

Fritz slapped his fist into his hand. "I knew I shouldn't have let you go out alone," he said. He laid his coat around my shoulders and led me over to the woodstove.

I stretched out my hands, grateful for the warmth that spread over them. The kids clustered around me, their faces serious in the flickering light. Suddenly I realized how dependent they all were on me. From now on I would have to be much more careful, for their sake as well as my own. Finally I said, "I'm all right, I really am." And the girls hugged me.

Fritz went over and picked up the bucket I had dropped near the door. "I'll get the water," he said.

Rudy jumped up. "I'll go with you," he said, "and I'll break the neck of any G.I. with a gash on his forehead."

Dieter and I got supper ready. He managed to open the can of stew with his army knife, and we set it on the stove to heat. I stirred it occasionally with a rusty spoon I'd found in the kitchen. By the time Rudy and Fritz returned, our meal was hot and ready to eat.

"I've got a surprise!" said Fritz, holding up a loaf of black bread. "For breakfast tomorrow," he added.

Chapter Ten

Then he turned to Dieter. "That's the last of our marks," he said quietly. Dieter nodded, patting him on the shoulder.

We all sat down cross-legged on the floor near the stove because our drying clothes were strewn all over the chairs. We had no plates and only the one spoon, so we decided to push the hot can of stew along the floor to take turns eating from it.

"Let's each eat two spoonfuls and then push it on to the next person," I said. I wrapped a shirt around the hot can and set it down in front of Volfie. It was a game to him, and he giggled as he lifted up each spoonful.

When it was the girls' turn, they ate slowly, savoring each chunk of potato or carrot. There wasn't much meat, but even the gravy was something none of us had eaten for months.

Rudy managed to fill the spoon as high as possible during his turn, and he glanced over at me guiltily. I started to say something, but Fritz interrupted. "It's all right, Rudy," he said. "Boys your age need a lot of food. I remember when I was thirteen. We never had any leftovers at the supper table."

The supper table. It had been more than two years since we had sat around the table as a family. Sometimes it seemed even longer than that.

"Will we be a family again soon?" asked Heidi, hugging her knees. She must have been thinking the same thing I was.

"We *are* a family," I said, wiping my mouth and pushing the can over to Fritz.

"Only partly," replied Heidi. "We need Papa and Christa and Hanna and the baby," said Heidi.

"Irene's not a baby anymore," said Helga, crossing her arms. It seemed strange to have a sister none of us had ever even seen. How many times had I tried to imagine Mama leaning over that baby—shielding her with her body as the bomb hit. And the plaster falling, and the ceiling crashing down on Mama. . . .

The can went around twice, and then it was empty. We finished off the meal with a drink of water dipped up from the bucket. If anyone was still hungry, no one said anything, for we all knew we had to save the bread for breakfast. And we had only the tin of raw sugar and the little bag of flour left in my knapsack for the rest of tomorrow.

Later we worked out sleeping arrangements. Heidi and Helga got the bed, and I took the couch. The boys said they'd sleep with the soldiers on the straw.

"Good thing we have our duffel bags," said Fritz, winking at Volfie. "Soldiers always carry extra clothes. We can use them for blankets." He pulled a heavy wool jacket out of his bag. Dieter got out his also. Between the two of them, they produced enough coats and jackets to cover all of us during the night.

Everyone was tired, so we soon went to bed, sleeping in our clothes once again. The room became quiet, and I lay in the dark listening to my sisters breathing. They must have fallen asleep immediately. I wasn't so lucky. Hard as I tried not to think about it, I kept seeing the soldier grabbing me in the alleyway.

What if I hadn't had the courage to swing at him? Where would I be now? And what would have happened to my brothers and sisters without me?

Even though it must have been quite late, the room was not totally dark. A thin light was coming in through the bare window. I got up, padded across the room, and peeked out through the grimy glass. After all the rain, only a few wispy clouds remained in the sky. A huge full moon flooded the yard like a spotlight.

I had a sudden urge to go outside where I'd be closer to all that beauty, but I didn't dare venture out by myself. I stayed by the window, thinking again about the close call I'd had that evening. And then, in the silence with everyone asleep, I suddenly felt surrounded by Something, or Someone. Could it be true after all? I wondered. Has Someone really been looking out for us all along?

I shook off the feeling and returned to bed, but I slept more soundly than I had since we left Schwandorf.

Chapter 11

1945

Thursday Morning, June 7

We all woke early the next morning, eager for the last day of our journey. We dressed in the clothes that had dried during the night, and I braided the girls' hair and my own. After so long a time without shampoos, braids at least made us look presentable.

When everything was packed and ready to go, we stood around the table while Fritz divided the black bread he'd bought the day before. It was coarse and nourishing, and there was enough for all of us to feel satisfied. Besides, at that point I think we were too excited to eat very much.

We hiked back up to the town hall and found the constable. "Thank you, Herr Koontz," said Fritz, placing the key in his hand.

"Better weather for traveling today," said the constable, tucking the key into his pocket. He walked with us back out onto the sidewalk. "Where did you say you're headed?"

"The children will go northwest to Waldeck," said Fritz. "My buddy and I are heading for Hamburg."

"You might find a train to Hamburg from here," said Herr Koontz. He looked over at me and shook his head. "Only way to Waldeck, though, is to walk or catch a ride. Problem is, no one can get any gas these days."

I nodded. How well we knew that. "How much farther?" I asked.

Herr Koontz scratched his head. "On foot? Most of the day," he said.

Rudy and I looked at each other. "We'll make it," I said, wishing I could be more sure of it.

"Waldeck is a nice town," added the constable, as we turned to leave. "There used to be a beautiful stone church right in the center of it with a golden dome—if it's still standing."

We thanked him again and started on our way.

The street and the houses looked soaked and scrubbed after all the rain. Early morning sunlight sparkled on the red tile roofs, and a brisk breeze pushed us playfully from behind, as if it were trying to help us along. The others were in good spirits with the end of our journey so near. I tried to match their mood but found myself watching the streets closely, afraid that someone might jump out and grab me.

Near the train station, the road forked, and we knew from our map that we would have to continue from here without Fritz and Dieter. We stopped and stood about awkwardly for a few moments.

"Well, kids," said Fritz, setting down his duffel bag, "this is it."

As soon as he said that, my eyes started smarting. "You were such a help to us," I said to Fritz and Dieter, shaking their hands.

"Our pleasure," said Dieter, touching his cap.

"Maybe you can come and see us sometime," said Heidi, pulling Fritz down for a hug.

"Sometime, maybe, yes," he replied, as he and Dieter hugged each of us in turn.

Finally Fritz straightened up and looked at me. "If you ever get to Hamburg, come and see us," he said.

"But you don't know where you'll be, and we don't know where we'll be."

He nodded. "But maybe somehow. Remember: Fritz Kriner and Dieter Braun. We'll be in the phone book someday."

"Someday," I repeated softly.

The soldiers heaved their bags onto their shoulders and tramped off toward the railway station, turning to wave as they went. We stood and watched, waving until they were out of sight.

The road led us out into the countryside. The immense sweep of sky was brilliant blue, and the sun warmed our backs and the roadbed, making it shimmer in the distance.

After we had walked a long while, Volfie started lagging behind. "Wait," he said, sitting down in some dry grass on the roadside. "I'm tired."

One by one we plunked down alongside him, glad

for a break. While we were sitting there, a dark green jeep came into sight far down the road. I stiffened.

"A ride!" shouted Rudy, jumping up. He and Volfie scrambled to their feet and started waving their arms. I sat back with my arms crossed.

The jeep slowed down somewhat, and a smiling soldier leaned out and tossed something toward us as he flew past. Rudy snatched it up from the ground. "A chocolate bar!" he said. It was the first one we'd seen in years. We stared at it in disbelief. He tore off the brightly colored wrapper, and we looked down at the smooth, brown bar, scarcely believing our eyes.

"I want some!" said Volfie.

"Me, too," cried Heidi and Helga.

Rudy snapped it into five even pieces, and we sat down again to enjoy the candy. Each of us was in our own private world, savoring our chocolate for as long as we could. I'd almost forgotten the taste of it. I let each tiny bite dissolve in my mouth before taking another. This unexpected treat, after years of potatoes and bread, seemed miraculous.

We continued walking until the sun was high overhead and a truck came chugging along, another wood-burner. To our delight it stopped in response to our arm-waving.

"Want a lift?" called the driver.

"Yes, please," we cried.

"I can take you as far as Frankenau," he said.

"That's right on our way," I replied. From our map, Frankenau looked very close to Waldeck.

The back of the truck was crowded with milk cans.

Before we found places to sit, the truck started up with a
lurch that threw us backward. Volfie hit his forehead on one
of the metal cans and started to cry.

I moved over and cradled him with my arm. "Let
me take a look," I said, brushing aside the shock of hair that
covered his brow. "It's swollen," I said, "and a little bruised,
but it's not bleeding."

"It hurts a whole lot," he grumbled. He kicked at the
milk can in front of him. "I'm sick of this."

"Of what?"

"Operation Morningstar. It's no fun. All we ever do
is walk. I can't walk anymore."

"But you don't have to walk now."

"But we will. I wish we'd never left."

"Volfie!" said Heidi. "Don't say that!"

"I mean it! I wish we had stayed in Schwandorf."

"Think about Papa, Volfie," I said. "We're getting
closer to him all the time." *If Papa is still alive,* I thought.

At two o'clock we reached Frankenau, and everyone
was hungry. I had planned by then what I would do with
the flour and raw sugar in my knapsack. At the nearest
pump, I took out the tin of sugar and allowed a dribble of
water to soak into it. Then, after we found a grove of trees
on the outskirts of the town, I took a stick and stirred the
sugar and water until it became a tan-colored syrup.
Gradually I added flour from the little sack until the mixture became very thick and doughy.

Helga watched as I stirred. "Looks like Mama's
cookies before she baked them," she said.

I brushed a wisp of hair out of my eyes. "Well," I

said, "we always liked to sample Mama's cookie dough, so let's pretend that's what this is." I handed a sticky ball to each of them.

Rudy winked at me as he took his dough. "Raw sugar saves the day," he said. He had salvaged it from a wrecked freight car back in Schwandorf. Word of the spilled sugar had spread among the hungry villagers like wildfire. By the time Rudy raced down to the wreck with his rusty tin, the sugar had all but disappeared. But what he did get had given us our last meal.

My own gooey lump tasted better than I had hoped. I smiled to myself, proud that the mixture had turned out to be almost pleasant. I just wished there were more of it.

"I'm still hungry," whined Volfie. "I want something else to eat."

"There isn't anything else, Volfie," said Rudy gently.

"But I'm still hungry!"

"Sorry," I said to him, "but we'll just have to wait until we get to Waldeck." I put the empty flour sack and tin down into my pack.

Volfie kicked at a gnarled tree root. "This is stupid!" he said.

Rudy looked over at him. "What's stupid?"

"This whole trip. It's stupid!"

"It is not," said Rudy. Next to me, Rudy had been the most eager to go to Waldeck, and I could see his face starting to flush.

"It is!" Volfie continued. "I wish we'd never gone!"

"Oh, shut up, Volfie," said Rudy, rolling his eyes.

Volfie swung at him. "Shut up yourself!" he said.

"Cut it out, Volfie!" said Rudy, grabbing his arm.

Volfie lunged at Rudy, knocking him backward onto the ground. They began to tussle.

"Stop it!" I cried, trying to pry them apart. "Stop it, both of you!"

Volfie sprang up. He ran to the middle of the road and turned to face us, fists clenched. "I'm leaving!" he cried.

Rudy laughed. "Go ahead, Volfie! Why don't you?"

Volfie spun around and headed back down the road.

"Volfie!" I yelled.

"Let him go," said Rudy, brushing himself off. "He won't go far."

We all stood and watched, expecting Volfie to turn around, but he didn't. He kept running down the road, farther and farther away from us.

Helga stood with her hands on her hips. "He'd better come back," she said. "We're wasting time."

Volfie slowed down, but he kept on walking. We waited, but he just became smaller and smaller. Then the road dipped, and he disappeared from sight.

Chapter 12

1945

Thursday Afternoon

"Wait here," I told Rudy and the girls. I took off down the road after Volfie, faster than I had ever run in my life. *Oh God,* I thought, *why did this have to happen?* And so near the end of our trip! I ran on and on.

Finally I reached a rise in the road where I could see far ahead. Volfie was nowhere in sight. Nowhere. I stood with my fists against my wet cheeks. "Please, God," I prayed, "please help us! We can't go on without Volfie!" And that's when I saw my little brother, sitting in dappled shade under a roadside tree.

"Volfie!" I cried, running toward him. "Volfie!"

Volfie slumped down and buried his face in his arms. He looked so wretched—straggly hair down to his shoulders, and rumpled, soiled clothing befitting a beggar. When I reached him, I sank to the ground and threw my arms around his bony little body. "Volfie," I said, hugging him hard.

He shook his head and struggled to free himself.

I dropped my arms. "I know you're mad at Rudy," I said, "but he's sorry. We all are."

He looked up. Tears had made shiny tracks down his dusty cheeks. "Why does Rudy always have to pick on me?" he said, brushing his nose with the back of his hand. "I can't help it if I'm still hungry."

I sat back on my heels, thinking fast. "We're all hungry, and tired too," I said. "But think how close we are to Waldeck! We have to keep going!"

"Then go by yourselves."

"We can't. We need you!" Then I added softly, "And you need us."

Volfie tossed his head and looked away.

"Think of Papa," I pleaded. "We'll be with Papa again!"

"We might not even find him."

"Of course we'll find him! One way or another, we'll all be together again!"

He sat biting his lip, and finally he looked back at me. "You really think we'll find Papa?" he asked.

"Cross my heart, Volfie." For the first time since we left Schwandorf, I actually believed it myself.

"And he will take us home?"

"Absolutely!"

I took his rough little hand into mine, and together

we started back up the road. Thank God he didn't resist.

Later that afternoon we reached a ridge overlooking a distant town, and in the center of the town stood a beautiful stone church with a golden dome.

"Waldeck!" we said. "It's Waldeck!"

All of us just stood there for a minute. The town was no longer just a dot on the map; it was finally real. Bathed in late afternoon sunlight, even the church walls looked like gold. None of us could run at that point, but just seeing it gave us the strength to walk a little farther. And Volfie led the way!

On the outskirts of town, a farmer was cutting hay. "Excuse me," I called to him. "Can you help us?" I tucked a stray wisp of hair back behind my ear.

The man set down his scythe and came over to the fence. He looked us over quickly and said gently, "You look like you've come a long way. What can I do for you?"

We told him about our sisters and how we'd heard they were on a farm near Waldeck.

"This is Waldeck, all right," said the farmer, wiping his brow with a large handkerchief. "Let's see, seems to me I heard about some children staying with a couple named Schneider." He took off his straw hat and scratched his head. "They're north of here. Took in three young ones a few months ago—little girls they were."

I felt my breath catch in my throat.

The farmer looked us over again and said, "You don't look like you could make it over there. Wait here, and I'll hitch up the wagon."

In a few minutes we were clop-clopping into town.

We drove right past the gold-domed church, which was surrounded by large houses of whitewashed stone. This was another town that had escaped the bombings.

As we rode, I thought about all the people who had helped us since we left Schwandorf: Frau Schmidt, the Americans in Herrsbruck, the nuns, Fritz and Dieter, the Red Cross, the woman with the can of stew, the constable, and now this farmer. All of them had come just when we needed them, after we had done all we could by ourselves. *That must be it!* I thought. *God does help us, but we have to do the best that we can do, too.* Suddenly I felt warm all over and cared for—as if Mama had just tucked me in for the night.

Our wagon turned at a crossroad and headed up a lane to a rambling farmhouse. A large collie lay on the porch, and when we approached, he stood up and started barking.

A heavyset, aproned woman came out of the house. "Hush, King!" she said, as she lumbered down the porch steps. The dog followed, wagging his tail.

"Are you Frau Schneider?" asked the farmer, pulling on the reins.

"Yes," she replied, looking at us curiously.

"These are the Mueller children. . . . "

"Mercy!" she said, clapping her hands to her face. "It's a miracle!" She ran back up the steps, shouting, "Peter! They're alive! Come quick!"

"Peter" was Papa!

"He's here?" I gasped, scrambling down from the wagon. The others followed excitedly.

"Just came for his little girls," she said. "They would

have been gone by now, but little Irene was sick all last week. Oh, I can hardly believe this is happening. . . ."

The door flew open, and Papa rushed toward us, looking as though he might faint. "My children! Oh, thank God!" he cried. He fell to his knees, and we tumbled into his arms, a family at last.

"How did you find us?" Papa asked, finally.

"We had lots of help," I told him, smiling through my tears. "Heavenly help." And Heidi and I winked at each other.

History in Real Life: World War II

Germany in the 1920s and '30s, like much of the world, experienced an economic depression, that resulted in unemployment, hunger, and homelessness. In 1921, a man named Adolf Hitler formed a political group called the Nazi party. When he was named to head Germany in 1932, he promised that he would put an end to the people's sufferings, which he blamed mainly on Jews and Communists. In 1934, he became Germany's absolute dictator, calling himself the *Führer* (leader).

Hitler dreamed of a great German empire in Europe, so in 1938 and 1939, respectively, he ordered the army to take over Austria and Czechoslovakia. The German army also invaded Poland in 1939, causing England and France to declare war on Germany.

For a while the Germans were very successful in their campaign to conquer Europe. They invaded Norway, Denmark, Holland, Belgium, France, Yugoslavia, Romania, Hungary, Greece, and western Russia (then the Soviet Union).

Then, in December 1941, the Japanese bombed Pearl

Harbor, an American naval base in Hawaii. The United States declared war on Japan immediately afterward. Because Germany had a treaty with Japan, Germany and the United States declared war on each other as well.

With the United States involved in what was by then called World War II, the tide was beginning to turn against Hitler and the Germans. The Allies (those countries which opposed Hitler) began to bomb German factories and oil refineries. They invaded countries in North Africa as well as Italy, which Germany had also taken over. Then, in 1944, the Allies invaded France, pushing the Germans back at the same time that the Russians were advancing from the other direction. Finally, in 1945, the Germans surrendered (Hitler had committed suicide), and their country was occupied by American, British, French, and Russian soldiers.

By the time of its defeat, Germany was in chaos. Millions had been killed, and most cities were in ruins. There was very little food and hardly any way for people to travel. Worse, no telephones were working, and mail service had stopped, making it almost impossible for separated family members to contact each other. It was under these conditions that the five Mueller children began their desperate journey across Germany, hoping to find what remained of their family.

Read More about It

To find out more about the World War II, check your local library for these titles:

Fiction

Lowry, Lois. *Number the Stars*. Boston: Houghton Mifflin, 1989.
    In 1943, during the German occupation of Denmark, ten-year-old Annemarie learns how to be brave when she helps shelter her Jewish friend from the Nazis. Newberry Award winner.

Matas, Carol. *Code Name Kris*. New York: Scribner, 1990, 1989.
    After his Jewish friends flee the country, seventeen-year-old Jesper continues his work in the underground resistance movement. Sequel to *Lisa's War*.

Matas, Carol. *Lisa's War*. New York: C. Scribner's Sons, 1987.
    During the Nazi occupation of Denmark, Lisa and other teenage Jews become involved in an underground resistance movement.

McSwigan, Marie. *Snow Treasure*. Dutton, 1942.
    A story, based on truth, of how a group of children smuggled gold out of Norway on their sleds during the German occupation of their country in World War II.

Nostlinger, Christine. *Fly Away Home*. New York: F. Watts, 1975.
    A young girl recalls what life was like for her family in Vienna toward the end of World War II.

Paton Walsh, Jill. *Fireweed*. New York: Farrar, Straus & Giroux, 1970, 1969.
Two teenage runaways who refuse to be evacuated from London, struggle to survive the blitz of 1940.

Nonfiction

Meltzer, Milton. *Rescue: the Story of How Gentiles Saved Jews in the Holocaust*. New York: Harper & Row, 1988.
A retelling of individual acts of heroism during the Holocaust.

Reiss, Johanna. *The Upstairs Room*. New York: HarperCollins, 1972.
A Dutch Jewish girl describes the two-and-one-half years she spent in hiding in the upstairs bedroom of a farmer's house during World War II.

Richter, Hans Peter. *I Was There*. Holt, 1972.
Eyewitness account of Hitler's rise to power and the author's involvement in "Jungvolk" (Hitler youth).

Rubenstein, Joshua. *Adolf Hitler*. New York: F. Watts, 1982.
The biography of a struggling Austrian artist who rose to be the head of the German nation.

Siegal, Aranka. *Grace in the Wilderness: After the Liberation, 1945-1948.* New York: Farrar, Straus & Giroux, 1985.
Liberated from a German concentration camp at the end of World War II, fifteen-year-old Piri starts a new life as a Jew in Sweden.

Snyder, Louis Leo. *World War II.* New York: F. Watts, 1981.
Spotlights the important events and people of World War II.

About the Author

Dorothy Lilja Harrison has loved hearing and reading stories ever since she was a little girl. Later, when she grew up and had two boys and two girls of her own, she shared her love of books with her children, as well as with the kindergartners she taught. Now, she has taken that love to the next level—she has authored the books of the Chronicles of Courage series.

At about that same time, Mrs. Harrison met a member of her church in Bethesda, Maryland, who had lived in Germany during World War II. When she heard Heidi's courageous story, she thought that children would love to hear about it too. *Operation Morningstar,* therefore, is about real people, and it is also almost entirely true.

Today Mrs. Harrison lives in Ellicott City, Maryland, with her husband, a retired United Methodist pastor. Their grown children have become a musician, an artist, an editor, and a nurse. Their two grandchildren live nearby.

A Better Tomorrow?

A snake in the kitchen?!

It seems the perfect revenge, but Janet's not sure she should go through with it.

Before the Depression, the Larsons had their own house and yard and were able to play with their friends whenever they wanted. Now Janet and her family are living with a cranky older woman named Mrs. Cooper who doesn't seem to like kids. She has very strict rules about having friends over, which hasn't made it easy for Janet to make new friends. She's tired of Mrs. Cooper and her rules, and she just wants to get even. But what does God want her to do?

Janet knows the Depression won't last forever, that God will bring a better tomorrow and she will have friends again. She just doesn't expect Mrs. Cooper to be one of them.

Be sure to read all three books in the
Chronicles of Courage series:
A Better Tomorrow?
Operation Morningstar
Gold in the Garden

ChariotVICTOR
PUBLISHING
A DIVISION OF COOK COMMUNICATIONS

Gold in the Garden

Death was not something I had thought about very much ... at least not until Susan died.

Kathy Jordan has a secret, one she is sure she can never tell. Her best friend, Susan, has died, and she believes it's her fault. If she tells anyone, she's sure she'll never have a friend again. After all, how could anyone—even God— love a person who caused her best friend's death?

A tender story of healing and forgiveness, *Gold in the Garden* reaches back to the days of the early 1950s when polio swept the nation. Many parents feared for the lives of their children. As you read, you'll discover along with Kathy that healing is possible for even the worst wounds of the heart.

Be sure to read all three books in the
Chronicles of Courage series:
A Better Tomorrow?
Operation Morningstar
Gold in the Garden

ChariotVICTOR
PUBLISHING
A DIVISION OF COOK COMMUNICATIONS

Home on Stoney Creek

"Kentucky! Why do we have to move to Kentucky?"

The cry for freedom is spreading throughout the colonies calling many people to war, but not Sarah's family. The cry they hear leads them to a new, untamed wilderness called Kentucky.

Sleeping on pine boughs covered with deerskins, having no one her age to talk to, fighting off pig-eating bears—Kentucky doesn't feel much like freedom to Sarah. She can't understand why God didn't answer her prayers to stay in Virginia, but she vows she'll return some day.

Wanda Luttrell was raised and still lives on the banks of Stoney Creek. Wanda and her husband have shared their home on Stoney Creek with their five children.

Be sure to read all the books in Sarah's Journey:
Home on Stoney Creek
Stranger in Williamsburg
Reunion in Kentucky
Also available as an audio book:
Home on Stoney Creek

ChariotVICTOR
PUBLISHING
A DIVISION OF COOK COMMUNICATIONS

Stranger in Williamsburg

"A spy? Gabrielle Can't be a spy!"

The American Revolution is in full swing, and Sarah Moore is caught right in the middle of it. When she returned to Virginia to live with her aunt's family and learn from their tutor, she certainly had no plans to get involved with a possible spy.

With a war going on, her family back in Kentucky, and people choosing sides all around her, Sarah has begun to wonder if she can trust anyone—even God.

Wanda Luttrell was raised and still lives on the banks of Stoney Creek. Wanda and her husband have shared their home on Stoney Creek with their five children.

Be sure to read all the books in Sarah's Journey:
Home on Stoney Creek
Stranger in Williamsburg
Reunion in Kentucky
Also available as an audio book:
Home on Stoney Creek

Chariot VICTOR
PUBLISHING
A DIVISION OF COOK COMMUNICATIONS

Grandma's Attic Series

Pieces of Magic

Remember when you were a child—when all the world was new, and the smallest object a thing of wonder? Arleta Richardson remembers: the funny wearable wire contraption hidden in the dusty attic, the century-old schoolchild's slate which belonged to Grandma, an ancient trunk filled with quilt pieces—each with its own special story—and the button basket, a miracle of mysteries. And best of all was the remarkable grandmother who made magic of all she touched, bringing the past alive as only a born storyteller could.

Here are those marvelous tales—faithfully recalled for the delight of young and old alike, a touchstone to another day when life was simpler, perhaps richer; when the treasures of family life and love were passed from generation to generation by a child's questions . . . and the legends that followed enlarged our faith.

Arleta Richardson has written the beloved Grandma's Attic series as well as the Orphans' Journey series. She lives in California where she continues writing and public speaking.

Be sure to read all the books from Grandma's Attic:

In Grandma's Attic
More Stories from Grandma's Attic
Still More Stories from Grandma's Attic
Treasure from Grandma

Chariot VICTOR
PUBLISHING
A DIVISION OF COOK COMMUNICATIONS

The Grandma's Attic Novels

At home in North Branch— what could be better?

The Grandma's Attic Novels bring you the story of Mabel O'Dell's young adult years as she becomes a teacher, wife, and mother. Join Mabel and her best friend, Sarah Jane, as they live, laugh, and learn together. They rise to each occasion they meet with their usual measure of hilarity, anguish, and newfound insights, all the while learning more of what it means to live a life of faith.

Arleta Richardson has written the beloved Grandma's Attic series as well as the Orphans' Journey series. She lives in California where she continues writing and public speaking.

Be sure to read all the Grandma's Attic novels:

Away from Home

A School of Her Own

Wedding Bells Ahead

At Home in North Branch

New Faces, New Friends

Stories from the Growing Years

ChariotVICTOR
PUBLISHING
A DIVISION OF COOK COMMUNICATIONS

Parents

Are you looking for fun ways to bring the Bible to life for your children?

ChariotVictor Publishing has hundreds of books, toys, games, and videos that help teach your children the Bible and show them how to apply it to their everyday lives.

Look for these educational, inspirational, and fun products at your local Christian bookstore.